DEAR IBIS

Spineless Wonders
PO Box 220 STRAWBERRY HILLS
New South Wales, Australia, 2012

shortaustralianstories.com.au

First published by Spineless Wonders in 2021
Text copyright © Kate Liston-Mills
Cover illustration and book design by Bettina Kaiser.

Edited by Jess Magrath. Copyediting and proofreading by Matilda Gould.

Typeset in Adobe Garamont Pro and Erbar Neo mini D

Printed and bound by Ingram Spark

Distribution in Australia and New Zealand by New South

Dear Ibis/ Kate Liston-Mills
ISBN 978-1-925052-61-9

A catalogue record for this book is available from the National Library of Australia

PRAISE FOR 'THE WATERFOWL ARE DRUNK!'

'Kate Liston-Mills' debut collection of fiction is an astute, often moving study of three generations of a small-town family. Set in the author's native Pambula in regional NSW, it captures the idiosyncrasies of rural life, using colloquialisms to render a complex portrait of outwardly simple stories… With Lottie as the book's focal point, Liston-Mills is able to demonstrate the fluidity of relationships over time, exploring the space between carer and cared-for, parent and child, love and resentment.'

MYLES MCGUIRE, Books + Publishing

'The book's apparent slightness and whimsical title belie the close observation and deep feeling that inform its contents… The stories follow a small cast of characters over two generations, drilling down into the details of daily life. The two standouts are narrated by Georgia, who is a teenage surfer dutifully visiting her grandmother, her attitude summed up in the title, *I Don't Even Like Scotch Fingers…*'

KERRYN GOLDSWORTHY, Sydney Morning Herald, The Age

'A short story can be defined as a short piece of prose, with few characters and a single theme. Often there is no common thread within a collection. Kate Liston-Mills has achieved the effect of a novel in *The Waterfowl Are Drunk!*. In episodic flashes, we follow the lives of Ed and Hazel, their children and grandchildren, and their friends and neighbours in the isolated town of Pambula. It's like looking through a photo album, but with the benefit of Liston-Mills' beautiful writing filling in some gaps, while sparking our imagination to fill in the rest.'

ROBERT FAIRHEAD, The NSW Writers Centre

'Disarmingly Aussie, pairing difficult issues with humour, laconicism and domesticity.'

BRIDGET LUTHERBORROW, Slinkies Curator

'Kate Liston-Mills' lush but precise prose and fresh perspective gives this collection about the tough stuff of ordinary life immense energy, beauty and warmth. That she manages to get depth of character and intense sense of place in such a slim collection is a true wonder, as is her ability to show the inherent drama and tragedy of everyday life without ever straying into sentimentality or bleakness.'

EMILY MAGUIRE, Author of *An Isolated Incident, Fishing for Tigers, Smoke in the Room*...

'Kate is a veritable Nigella Lawson of letters, unable to resist tiptoeing down to the fridge after midnight to indulge in one more simile, one more metaphor. And what delicacies she has crafted in this smorgasbord, what moments of descriptive brilliance, masterful details and turns of phrase slipped expertly into the narrative... Working in the best traditions of the tall tales and urban myths repeated and embellished in country pubs the nation over, *The Waterfowl Are Drunk!* is a richly rendered and skillful meditation on birth, death and disability in coastal, regional New South Wales.'

L PHILLIP LUCAS, Author of *The Innocuous Death of Irving Crabbe*

'While *The Waterfowl Are Drunk!* can be seen as an easy weekend read, a nice escape to small-town Australia, there's plenty of poetry to give poise to the robust language and difficult themes. Liston-Mills balances literary technique with story and character in a way that is appealing to a wide audience, crafting a collection that stirs nostalgia with its authenticity and Australiana beauty.'

WRITER'S EDIT

'*The Waterfowl Are Drunk!* is a poetic treasure. Kate Liston-Mills has captured the intimacy and isolation of rural Australian life. Unlike anything I've read before, heartbreakingly funny, vivid and moving.'

MEGHAN BREWSTER, Author of *How To Heal A Bruise* and *Bellies, Babies And Bruises*.

PRAISE FOR 'DEAR IBIS'

'This book is its own birdcall, magnificent and rich with 'moments of union' between the human and the non-human world. Liston-Mills is irrepressible in this celebration of being alive with each other. She is a superb storyteller and defiant poet. Her words leap from image to insight, to look us in the eye. We cannot look away. We are transfixed by love and loneliness, greed and grit, cruelty and care, and all the clutter of being human — but always there is the joy of 'bird friends' or of simply being bird.'

MERLINDA BOBIS, Author of *Locust Girl: A Lovesong* and *Rita's Lullaby*

'*Dear Ibis* is a collection of stories that reminds us what it means to be human. It captures the grace and heartache of being alive for a brief moment on a beautiful planet. Kate Liston-Mills' characters are so tactile they could be our neighbours, our lovers, ourselves. She has captured the extraordinary lurking in the ordinary with her use of detail and nuance. This collection offers one stunner short story after another. You will leave this book a better person for having spent time with these characters and their lives.'

SHADY COSGROVE, Author of *She Played Elvis* and *What the Ground Can't Hold*

'This is an extraordinary collection: sad and funny, lonely and defiant, devastating and regenerative. Liston-Mills shows us the deep wounds we inflict on each other and our environment, but also the moments of lightest joy: the call of a bird in the empty air, the song of a child in the house next door. These stories are places of hope and of change, where we all belong.'

JOSHUA LOBB, Author of *Flight of Birds: A Novel in Twelve Stories*

'A magnificent, kaleidoscopic vision of tenderness and love, told with courage, humour and precision.'

CHRISSY HOWE, Author of *Song in the Dark*

Author's Biography

Kate Liston-Mills is a writer, educator and librarian from the Far South Coast of NSW. Liston-Mills has worked as a journalist for both regional and urban publications and has had short stories, reviews and poetry published in various Australian journals and anthologies. She is the current host of Little Fictions on Air, a radio program that showcases the best of Australian short fiction. Her first major creative work, *The Waterfowl Are Drunk!* is an illustrated collection of short stories published with Spineless Wonders in 2016. *Dear Ibis* is its fiery sequel.

I acknowledge the traditional custodians of the lands on which this book was written, the people of the Yuin Nation. I pay my respects to ancestors and Elders past, present and emerging. Sovereignty has never been ceded. It always was and always will be Aboriginal Land.

For Ash ... the character and the human.

And for little River, my newest love.

Author's Note

Dear Ibis is a letter. Like all letters, it is a time capsule. Written during a year of fire, flood and a global pandemic, *Dear Ibis* touches on some of the key challenges that have impacted our world. Readers are advised that this book explores themes of mental illness, suicide, death, disability, colonialism, xenophobia, White privilege and the 2019/2020 Australian bushfire season. Please go gently if these themes are likely to be triggering for you.

Dear Ibis is a work of fiction. Names, characters, and incidents are products of the author's imagination or are used fictitiously. Any resemblance to actual events, or persons, living or dead, is entirely coincidental. That said, no work of fiction stands apart from the context in which it was written. In recognising the great privilege it is to write and publish a book such as this, I would like to take this opportunity to highlight some of the other voices I have found both instructive and inspiring in the many fields *Dear Ibis* traverses, including but by no means limited to: Behrouz Boochani's *No Friend but the Mountains*, Merlinda Bobis' *Locust Girl: A Lovesong*, Maxine Beneba Clarke's *The Hate Race*, Michael Mohammed Ahmad's *The Lebs*, Ashley Kalagian Blunt's *How to Be Australian*, Bruce Pascoe's *Dark Emu*, Tara June Winch's *The Yield*, Kirli Saunders' *Kindred*, and Ali Cobby Eckermann's *Inside My Mother*.

Above all, *Dear Ibis* has been a privilege – an opportunity to grapple with some of the big questions, both personal and political, that have dominated recent times. In offering up this book to you, dear reader, it is my sincere hope that whatever jolts of recognition, anger, sadness or reflection it may stir, we continue writing this letter together.

I am not the same person as I was before. That
cannonball came. I burnt up as I shot out. I floated
through time as if it was nothing but air. Heavy,
I plummeted. Connected to all sorts of feathery beasts,
I studied myself through a fabricated other. Paint
covered my wings at various points and I grieved ...
but then I rose, my feathers bright red, and I flew.

Dear Ibis, I wish you could see me now.

DEAR IBIS

KATE LISTON-MILLS

'I understood myself only after I destroyed myself.
And only in the process of fixing myself, did I know
who I truly was.'
Sade Andria Zabala

Contents

Cannonball

The day clings to the frosted grass, then slinks in like a vixen through the windows of Bernie's house. It's the sun that really sets him off. First thing, like a blooming bell. He pulls his corduroy pants up, reattaches his braces, and grunts. His body hasn't felt quite right lately. A bit off, actually. He shuffles into the bathroom and grips the vanity, steadies himself, and pauses while he catches his breath. He studies his washed-out face in the mirror, disgusted. How did he get this old? Fifty bloody two. Feels terrible. The sunspots all over his face look a bit deadly, a bit cancerous, he thinks. His moist eyes look back at him, alarmed. Fifty-two isn't this old, is it? He turns on his side and even though he tries not to see it, the lump on the back of his neck has grown. But maybe it's nothing.

He dabs some Brylcreem through his lengthy but thinning hair at the back and then combs the slick upwards to cover his bald bits. Like a spirited oil slick. An otter in a stream. Though there's no hair on top, you wouldn't know – that slick end comes up to say hello right at the forehead. Entranced by the length of this mullet and the magic of Brylcreem, Bernie forgets momentarily about the lump. The lump. Ah, that thing. Maybe it is nothing. Bernie nods at himself. He looks over at the picture of Marie sitting on the vanity. She would have made him go to the docs by now ... but he doesn't need no damn doctor telling him he's dying. Nup, no-one needs that.

The tiles are cold underneath his fat feet as he turns and shuffles to the door. The damn shop won't open itself. It's these diurnal rhythms that keep his mind from the lump and all its atrocities. The world's a stinking place. He's mumbling, but he doesn't even realise he's mumbling. *The world's a stinking place.*

As he passes the table, he glances at the unpaid bills and remembers the dream he'd had the other night, where a debt collector had knocked on his door. But when Bernie had gone to shake his hand, the debt collector had turned into the grim reaper. On seeing his cloak and scythe, Bernie turned to run and as he did the grim reaper vomited salt water all over him. It was the water that had woken him up, terrified.

He's not sure whether it's the mere thought of getting sick that has him spinning or whether he really is just spinning like a water mill, crazy, infected. He steadies himself and clumsily grabs at his name badge on the key hook by the door and fixes it to his blue shirt.

All this working and worrying and working and what's it all for? He's heard of people dying of tumours before. Ghastly time they all had. Old Harry down the road. Young Bessy next door ... back when Bernie was a youngster. Bloody great big lumps in their brain, in their underarms. *Damn bloody murderous things*, he mutters, heading out the door and into the paper shop. *Another bloody overcast day.* The door swings open easily beneath his hand ... he must have forgotten to lock it last night. He kicks the bundled papers in through the entrance and they skid across the wooden floor. Today's news. Bloody murder, he's sure. 'Tis the day for it. He tries to remember locking the door last night but he can't.

Memory's thrown it in too, he decides, as he pops open his till. Not much loot in here again. Not much of a float to start with. He flips the 'Closed' to 'Open' and catches sight of all the little handprints, grubby and smeared, on his front window.

'Damn little ...'

'How-ya, Bern?'

First customer, a merry man, bubbles into the paper shop and interrupts Bernie's muttering. But Willie the cobbler is too cheerful. *How damn delightful it must be to be Willie.* He shuffles behind the counter in case the upbeat energy can catch.

'Morning, Will ...'

'Bern, you don't look too flash. You alright, mate?' Willie leans in across the counter to get a closer look at Bernie's face.

He's done for. Even the bloody shoemaker can smell the death on him. Bernie runs his thumbs up and down, up and down his white braces, leaning backwards away from Willie's beaming face. He pulls out the corners of his blue shirt, just in case they are crinkled. He inflates his chest like a pigeon.

'In fact, I've never been better, Willie.'

Bernie pushes his sausage fingers through his slick of gelled hair, and looks down greenly at Willie's fancy boots.

'Rightio, then. Good, good. Just a Bombala Times and a Magnet please, good sir!'

Bernie cuts the bundle open and slides the two newspapers across the bench. With two fingers he slides Willie's pennies into the till. Clink, clink. The sound tinkles in his ears and makes him feel warm.

Willie examines the front page of the Magnet.

'Murder! *Bomb kills young family in Bega* ... a bomb of stolen gelignite ... killing a little babe, too ... well, that is a damn shame!

Just isn't our year, is it, Bern?'

He keeps reading at the counter as if Bernie isn't there.

'Ugh ... a constable too ... shame, shame. Alrighty, you take care now, Bern, won't you? Cheerio,' and he closes the paper, and lifts his hat.

As the door swings closed and the dust twirls in the air, Bernie's mood returns. Murder indeed! So everything *is* awful ... Bernie starts reading the tragic front page and feels a cavern of darkness opening up underneath him. He wants to be swallowed. He wills it. He mutters as he slips the different papers, all dripping with grim tidings, into their racks. *Bloody Willie-shoe-man, blooming nosy little blighter ... annoying happy clack-box ... all bloody hat and no bloody cattle ...*

Ed carefully places a big box of dynamite into Golden Bob's arms in the back of Bundy's ute. Nobel's dynamite. The best. Yellow gold.

'Goooone fishin', Haze!' Ed yells through the open front window.

Hazel doesn't hear him – she's busy with the girls, trying to break up fights over the cricket bat and trying to nurse Lottie and keep her from crying. You can see Haze's eye bags through the makeup. She's not slept more than a few hours a night going on three years now.

The ute lurches to the side and starts rolling down the hill, hardly even making a sound. Bundy managed to find some newer spark plugs last week and they've really made a world of difference. Golden Bob tries to anchor himself in one spot using his legs. His eyes don't move from the dynamite.

The men fire up. They start arguing about whether the Melbourne

Cricket Ground was actually the right place to hold the Olympics.

'Ruddy government shoulda paid for a bloomin' oval and extra hotdogs to be put 'ere in Pambula. We regionals never get no love from the pollies. I want them damn fancy dogs in ma belly,' Bundy yells.

'But Bund, I don't wanna pay no extra taxes! And I don't want crowds of ninnyhammers stuffing 'round my streets! They can stay in the damn city, the lotta them!'

'No, we shouldn't pay extra taxes, they should pay extra taxes … they get the better docs and shows and what not. For the love of God and the Queen, the 'lympics shoulda been 'ere!'

The ute winds around the dirt road and slows down just before the big bend. Golden Bob tries to move in sync with the vehicle, as if him and the blue ute are one. The dynamite sleeps in his arms like little babes, tired but volatile.

They pull off to the side and let the engine sputter to a stop. Bellbirds tinkle overhead, watching, always watching, from their hidden nooks in the trees. The river is a whirl of activity. Leaping mullet, flipping bream, curious toads all busy under the surface. None of the fish notice the ute's arrival. None of them know what's in the tray. The tide is in and the water's full of food and it's a race between fish and men.

The men heave themselves out of the low ute and breathe in the heavy air. It's sticky with summer, all soggy and sodden.

'But Bund, if they p-p-put a big stadium here in Pamby, alls them city folk would start m-moving here … And here just wouldn't be here anymore, you know w-whatta mean?'

Bundy picks up his gangrenous leg that seems to be still stuck under the steering wheel and levers it out of the ute. He stands up tall – and he still does somehow stand taller than the other two men, despite it. He looks at the deep river hole and its teeming life and continues.

'They don't wanna live 'ere! We's all riding horses and blowing fish up and making our own houses. They ain't got it in 'em!'

Ed grabs three of the yellow sausages from Golden Bob's box and lights them with a match. They crack and sizzle and he quickly flips them all into the water. The men laugh their heads off like little boys as they explode. All except Bundy. He just shudders a little, but Ed and Golden Bob don't notice. The water ripples as if Nessie itself is churning underneath. If it was a kettle it'd be whistling like a bush-stone curlew. Silver bellies start floating up. One. Two. Four. Seven. More. Some tiny buggers. Some enough for a good feed.

Golden Bob lights another two and waits a second extra than Ed. The men start yelping and hooting like puppies. And then the yellow boxes toss into the writhing river and don't explode. The men wait. Another half second. And then *boom, boom.* The water opens its lip and burps. Another big silvery belly floats up to the river's lip and hangs there suspended like a hot air balloon. The men chortle, imagining the fresh feeds they'll be eating tonight. Maybe they'll sell some. Make a buck or two. Why would you fish with a line when you can get a good spectacle and heaps more catch with a bang?

One by one the men start wading out to collect their catch. Ed swims out the furthest, because he's the best swimmer. The water grows more freezing the further out he goes. As he treads water his feet seem distant, like they belong to someone else. It's black down there. And he's sure the river holds secrets.

He throws two large-ish bream towards Bund and Bund then throws them up towards the riverbank. Golden Bob is collecting all the ones that have drifted in the tide upstream. He can see the silver bodies on the bank, glinting in the light. About 12, he thinks. Pretty good.

Ed looks ahead. One bream, one blown-up trevally in pieces, one rotten little toad. But there's something else floating there. Something like hair. Trails of ratty hair stringing through the water. Must be a dog or something ...

Ed keeps throwing the fish towards Bund. A raven *raaah-raaaahs* over in the wattle on the bank, and it sounds like a kiddy wailing. Ed looks over at it, disconcerted. *Sometimes birds sound so much like humans*, he thinks.

He nears the strange trail of dark hair. He can see the outline of a head, not a dog. He stops still in the icy water. They've killed someone. Without a doubt, they've blown someone up. A woman, for sure. Ed feels terror clutch at him as if he's a life raft. But he's no life raft. It's like he's forgotten how to swim, how to stay afloat. He lifts the head so it can breathe. But his hand trembles as it lifts.

The head is up just hanging above the surface in the fresh air and Ed quickly realises the skin is in sheets. Bloated, white sheets. Nothing that could have just happened. This is death from a week ago. Could death grab at him? Is it catchable? It's like something is dragging him down, his fear a weighty anchor dragging him into the blackness. His breath almost runs away across the surface of the river. He can see it it's so cold, and it almost escapes him. He tries to hold onto it. He tries to slow it down so he can speak.

'Oy, hoy! There's a ... there's a ... someone 'ere!'

Bundy and Golden Bob both look over and see the hairy thing. Their mouths hang.

Ed loses strength and dumps the head back into the water, as if it's bait. He treads water and sucks in air, trying to calm himself.

His thoughts are all beasts and birds and chaos. He clumsily knocks the back of the body under the water with his knee and hand, unsure. The spine is spiky, but the rest seems billowy.

Golden Bob has started swimming over like a burly frog, gluttonous, curious. Their hearts are thumping so loud they can see the bounce of it in their temples. It's all splashing and grunts for a few seconds. Golden Bob starts inspecting the body. Ed just stares, realising now up close, that it is a man, all faded white, almost blue, and curled over like a flower. Ed and Bob, together, turn him over. *One, two, three.* Now the face is up, dead to the world. Dark tendrils run down the cheeks like serpents. But this is no Medusa. This is definitely a portly man. They study the white braces against the blue shirt and they try to recognise something, anything.

With his tanned hands, Ed pulls the soft, waterlogged chin towards him. So white it's see-through. He studies the fishy marble eyes that stare fixated into the water. *Crikey*, he mutters. The dead man has still got his name badge on and Ed wonders whether he could have, would have, done this to himself. Surely not. Bernie the newspaper hawker, surely not.

Ed takes the back of the dead man's shirt in his hands. He tugs at it and drags it back towards shore. The hair floats on top of the water like algae. Ed notices the blue edges. Ol' Bern from the paper shop, deader than the fish, belly up, just floating.

It's like he's dragging a huge pile of phosphorescence. It takes all his strength. It seems to get heavier and bluer the closer to shore it gets. Ed's got a fever running through his arm. He's awash with adrenalin. He's rippling through the water like the dynamite and he's scared of what they've done, what this is, what's happened to Bernie. Golden Bob catches up and helps him pull. Bernie's still heavy like lead, even with the two of them.

The weight of a man … the weight of a man … they ponder.

Golden Bob, Bundy and Ed sit bundled on the bank. They hold their hats in their hands and stare down into the stones in silence. The distended fish all lay bellies up towards the sun, like sparkly tiles on a bathroom floor. And the swollen blue man is coiled up like a ball of wool, unravelling and fleshy on the bank. His feet are ribboned together by rope, rope that couldn't bear the bang.

A simple autopsy showed the man had a benign lump on his neck and that he died of drowning. They called the lump a lipoma and they called the death a suicide. Bernie from Bernie's Paper Shop, now with a front-page news story all of his own, had crawled down the bank almost a week ago. His raging fear tied a rope to a huge boulder and then to his own ankles so tight it had stung. He knotted it and he didn't like how the knot cut into his skin. His lips quivered and his head spun, but there was a heavy cape around his shoulders that urged him on. He rolled that boulder down the rock embankment so that it teetered over the deepest part of the river. A few bellbirds *chink-chinked* quietly from their boughs, which was the last sad sound his ears caught. Step by terrified step he pushed the rock further until it fell off the edge and plopped like a cannonball into the dark. It took Bernie with it, shoes first. He tried to clamber to the edges of the embankment, but it was all too rough and quick for him to catch onto anything. He was in the water in seconds. It was all cold … the air, the water, the night, the rope, the fear. He felt the boulder leave the first ledge and sink down into the next deep hole and he felt the rope around his legs cut further into his skin, pulling him under like a thief. It was dark when he went under and he could only see the silver licks of moon above him as he plunged further down. He looked up as he sank. Wondering. Wondering whether that lump really was the death of him. He felt the black blanket of fear eat him whole and fill his ears with a thick emptiness. And as the boulder stopped moving and his body found its resting place, not up or down but somewhere in limbo, he saw the glow of a disc above him, warped through the water, that faded out to nothing.

The Gull and the Space Junk

Nina sits on a banana chair at the beach, reading *Woman's Day*. Her grown-up daughter Georgia is out surfing, home for the uni holidays. Nina watches a group of teenagers bother a seagull, but she's not paying attention to the boys, or the gull, or the pangs in her weathered body. She's thinking of something else. Something like heaven, or the place we go after here. She wonders what tests there might be while she waits, or whether she has been tested enough ... but the squeals that curl from the boys' lips hit her thoughts with a dart and she becomes pinned to them, reluctantly.

They are trying to feed the gull a drug. They try catching the bird but the bird is too clever and it continues to evade them, flying high just as their sticky, adolescent fingers get near. Then it returns looking for chippies, scraps and beach-goer treats slightly further along the beach. Nina considers telling them off but the thought burns in her sternum like reflux. No, no, she'll stay here and pretend it is not happening. Besides, even if she did say something, it wouldn't change anything.

Her neck relaxes back against the plastic slats of her chair. The boys' voices become clearer with her eyes shut.

'Shit, Beau, get his legs, grab 'em!'

'Nah, he's too quick, hey. Let's put it in some food. That'll get him!'

Surely there are better things they could be doing with their time. She winces and can't avoid the déjà vu.

It is the school yard, Merimbula Public School, 1953, and Nina is trying to read her book.

'Oi, Reggie! That's nothin', look at mine …'

'No fair, no fair! Jack, move, let me see!'

'Henry, your eggs suck. You should see Col's …'

Nina tries to ignore the boys around her. Enid Blyton's *Five on a Treasure Island* rests open in her lap against her stockings. Her sister Sue is next to her, reading a different Blyton, not as distracted as Nina. Perhaps her book is more engrossing?

'You haven't got a bell miner's, I've got a bell miner's!' Reggie boasts, leaning backwards so his chest looks bigger.

'Move, move, let me in …'

'Bell miners are everywhere. Not that good, Reg. I've got a yellow thornbill's and a maggie's!'

Henry has garnered more attention with that comment and others squish in around Nina's sunny spot under the gum. Nina looks up at their greedy fingers all veiny and bent and eager as they compare their stolen goods. Her skirt now has dirty footprints all over it from the crowd.

'I can't see 'em. Move, Henry, let us in …'

Nina slams her book shut. She stands up full of tingle and huff and stomps over to the other side of the playground. Sue follows. No sun, no tree, just cold shade and damp. Nina looks back over and can see some younger girls have now joined the hullabaloo and she rolls her eyes.

On this day, Mr Mitchell signals the end of lunch early with a clanging ring of his metal bell. Confused, everybody trundles in and waits at the entrance to their little wooden-shack school, anxious to find out what has brought their playtime to a finish.

Nina truly believes Mr Mitchell is the smartest person to have ever walked the planet. As he puffs and huffs in front of the classroom door, she imagines all of his grand ideas like little hamsters running, wheeling and nestling into his brain pockets, waiting for that right moment to burst out. She can feel one of those great ideas about to break through the cage and scurry onto the floorboards. His mouth twitches and this is something he only does when he is very cross. She studies his skin folds, his sun spots, the hollows of his eyes, the way his hair turns grey around the ears. While he stands in front of her, waiting for quiet, she watches the worry tinker around his eyebrows and the crinkle in between them grow longer. She knows it won't be a happy hamster that drops onto the floor this time.

'It has come to my attention that you're all stealing eggs. This is very disappointing, very disappointing indeed ...' With that his eyes zone in on a group of boys at the back. He takes his wide brimmed hat off his head as if it is adding to his anger. 'Because of this, our bird numbers are dwindling. This must cease. You boys up the back listening?'

His voice is cutting. The boys around Nina all look at the dirt, their heads like empty sacks and their pockets clearly bulging with marbles and eggs.

'I never thought I'd see a day when my students would steal a mother's eggs!' Then he shakes his head as if trying to lose a fly. 'Do it again and there will be serious repercussions!'

Nina feels the shame of the others radiate through the back of her shirt like a heat bag. She has never been in trouble before and if she had an egg in her pocket right now, she is sure she would keel over and die from the guilty weight of it.

With fervour, Mr Mitchell swings open the door and strides

through. 'I've signed us up to the Gould League of Bird Lovers. It's a competition ...' he paces up and down in front of the chalkboard, scratching his temples; every step is heavy.

The students all file in.

'And maybe one day we'll go to the bird calling championships, a trip to the city if we play our cards right ...'

He stops at the blackboard and puts his hands on his hips. The kids sit down in their seats, conscious not to even let their chair legs squeak.

'From now on, we protect birds. We do not steal eggs. I'll be watching you all ...'

And as Mr Mitchell starts writing down the first verse of *Faces in the Street* by Henry Lawson on the chalkboard, the kids copy it without any prompting, bruised like they'd been walloped. Nobody speaks for the rest of the day. Just heads down, writing lines.

Over the next few weeks, Sue helps form the first bird calling committee and Nina helps her take the meeting minutes. Recess and lunch sounds become less shrieky and more hooty, as competition grows fiercer. Some kids get very good. Some connect with real birds. And the blowing out of an egg, the gut-churning slow drip of its insides, the quick gutting of the nests, all cease. Mr Mitchell is even surprised at the speed and ease of the transition and he puts it all down to the appeal of competition. Kids love to race. You just have to grab that energy and put it into something good. It is all in the way you market it.

Around the playground, kids have their mouths permanently pursed and pushed in all sorts of weird arrangements. Sometimes they use hands. Sometimes they bite their lips. Not many can master calls the first go. It's all trial and error. Some calls take weeks to master. Some calls seem impossible. But the birds come in their droves to feast on the newly-planted native trees and bushes, and the kids are continually listening and honing their craft. Mr Mitchell spends most lunchtimes trying to identify the call that sounds most like a mopoke. *Boo-book, boo-book, book-book.* Even Nina and Sue's hands bulge with muscles from cupping and flapping, and their pishing techniques eventually become better than most of the boys. Sue is particularly good at it. Reggie and Henry set up several ceramic feeder dishes around the playground and keep them filled with water. Fridays become planting day and every week the kids plant a couple more native shrubs to bring in the birds. It is a bustling schedule and that's not even including the bird hikes and excursions. Nina shares her time evenly between birds and books, birds and books ... lots of reading and *boo-booking* ... it's a dream life. Perhaps the best time she has ever had.

By the end of spring, red-haired Reggie gets so good at the magpie warble that he manages to call one right into the classroom. In it comes, with its unforgiving beak, its sharp antipodean eyes and its cheeky jumping along the windowsill. Maxie, they call him. A frequent visitor to the classroom windowsill, Maxie takes no notice of Mr Mitchell whenever he tries to shoo him away. His yodel grows so loud it often destroys Mr Mitchell's lessons.

By summer, Maxie rules the roost and that is the status quo. Sometimes on the weekends, Mr Mitchell even finds himself bringing Maxie treats and leftovers. Cheese, strips of meat – often the best, most expensive stuff he has. Nina and Sue catch him one day during the summer holidays, as they are walking to the shops with their mum and their little sister. He is bent over, positioning all kinds of expensive treats along the windowsill while trying to warble at Maxie. Nina and Sue smile but do not call out to him.

They pocket that memory like a little gem in their hearts.

Nina watches the gull finally eat the loaded bread and the beach bursts with sudden shadows. The boys whoop and whirl, tripping over their own feet in jubilation. She sighs, an empty sigh. If she was bigger, she would have said something. Wouldn't she? She's not sure. The boys sprint after the bird, necks straining from holding their stupid heads up. She sits upright in her plastic chair, trying to watch for the bird to explode or drop or disappear, but it fades into the mist before anything happens. All she can make out are the shapes of the boys hurtling like rockets into the distance.

Their screaming becomes inaudible and she tries to look for Georgia out in the surf, but the surfers all look the same in their wetsuits. All just floating seals, bobbing over the waves like fishing floats. Besides, Nina knows Georgia wouldn't be very good in this situation. She just seems to get angrier and angrier the more she studies. She feels every single pain of the world as if it is distinctively hers. She's now finishing her third degree and all the reading and work and critical examinations just make her volatile. It's a bit frightening sometimes and it often feels very personal. She's happy Georgia's out surfing, away from this moment. Of course she worries about her, so she likes her close. But just far enough away to not have to hear her. Everything is quieter when Georgia isn't here.

The gaggle of country kids squawk at the train station, hardly drawing breath. It's the biggest thing any of them have done. Shooting up to the city feels like they are shooting up into space. The train moves quicker than they were expecting. Nina remembers feeling hungry but not for food. She remembers Mr

Mitchell telling them to all sit down, umpteen times, as they tried to peer out the big windows. The trees and the mountains fly by, almost too quick for their eyes to grab hold of. But after a couple of hours, everyone starts to fidget. Fingernails are gnawed at. Swallows catch in their throats. This is a state-wide competition. They have no hope competing against fancy city kids. What were they thinking? What has Mr Mitchell thrown them into?

Nina looks down at her two tiny hands – their inferiority, poorness, palms all shaking and wet. She tries to cup them hard and fierce around each other to make the perfect goblet shape. She slightly adjusts the place where her hands overlap and then pushes the goblet to her face, searching for the perfect seal. She wants to make sure the smoggy city air is not going to rob her of her ability to do a mopoke call … and as she blows, she finds the air just releases into her cupped hands and warms them. No sound comes out. Is it too late to stop the train?

She watches the monstrous buildings zoom past through the window and she thinks of Dickens. She thinks of Lawson and Patterson and all the things she thought she knew about the city now quickly forming knots inside her tummy. The lustrous sheen of it all has well and truly come off.

Henry watches Nina fail to make a sound. He quickly cups his own hands as if they are playing Chinese whispers. He tries a mopoke call. It takes a while … a hoot does eventually escape but it is warblish, almost like an engine. They are done for.

Mr Mitchell feels the burgeoning fear of inferiority that plagues any country soul as they near the lights of a city. He's like a water bottle full of steam and regret. Words slip out of his wrinkled mouth that he regrets straight away … *So many people live in the city … the platform will be very, very crowded … the city is very dangerous ... people will be buzzing everywhere as if nobody but themselves matter ... there will be rubbish and grime and cockroaches and dangers that don't exist back home ...* He is fearmongering and he knows it. It feels ugly on him, but he can't help it. He had filled them up with wild dreams and air, and he can feel the balloon unknot and start to soar crazily around the carriage.

Out of his tattered bag he pulls an old bit of rope, about two metres long, and says that at all times the kids must have one hand on the rope. Without any reinforcement and well before the train even slows, the kids lean in towards the rope and grab hold of it as if they are going to breathe through it. The rope is life. The rope is hope. The group has nothing else to cling to.

As the train zooms through the darkness of a tunnel and the brakes screech to a halt, Nina feels like her body might explode like a cracker, so that she might turn to ash and float off into the air without a trace. That's her only hope at this point. But she doesn't dissolve or melt or ignite. She doesn't float away. The train wobbles for a few seconds. The doors slide open and the rope like a stem; the kids, like the flowers, bloom out and onto an empty platform. Apart from them, the platform is completely empty.

Nina remembers Mr Mitchell's sun-tanned face, all sallow and pasty. She remembers the rope, frozen in time, all their little beating hearts pulsing on the platform looking for life and finding none. There was not one person there.

That rope of flowers, rainbow against the grey backdrop, slowly moves up the stairs. The backdraft from the train and the tunnels blows up at them as they walk. Nobody speaks. The whole station is deserted as if the world has ended while they were on the train and only they have been left alive. Only this one little trail of 12 kids from the bush and their baffled teacher stand in that urban galaxy with their trembling dreams.

There is silence as they walk the many vacant tunnels of the station, clutching that brown rope 'til it frays in parts.

Nina remembers little callouses burning into her soft palms underneath the rope's clutches. The corridors were vacant and the green and white tiled columns stood beside them like giants.

As they near the final tunnel before the exit, something very wonderful happens. Teddy, a freckled older boy, with no warning at all, emits the male eastern whipbird's drawn-out whip crack of a call. Loud. Long. Exquisite in the acoustics of the long empty room.

Wooooooooooooooooo-whittt. Wooooooooooooooooooo-whitt.

The other boys one by one join in and the sound hits the concrete and reverberates around their feet, sizzles up the walls, rumbles overhead and fills their hearts with home. The girls answer the call with their *choooooo choooos* and it is a sound that has never lived in the underground before. It's as if its brilliance is amplified on the cement. It grows louder, and the kids feel they have finally found their stage. The sound they make feels like it could transcend the smells of old water dripping from the pipes, and the dusty air of the tunnels – a new language that could connect them. Connect them right back to home. Mr Mitchell weeps. And refills. Just in time for the crowds outside the station.

Thousands of people and their pounding cheers surround the outside of the station entrance. For a moment they think it's all for them. The holds on the rope tighten and as the rope of kids all near the entrance they can make out an elaborate train stopped on the tracks with what looks like Queen Elizabeth II and Prince Phillip waving at the front.

Thousands of hands wave, and as the kids get closer they fail to see anything in front of them, or behind them. The rope becomes survival and their moment of transcendence has come to an end.

'No wonder there was nobody in the station,' Mr Mitchell yells to them, 'Hold tight now, kids, hold tight! We're in the presence of royalty!'

And their minds blow like bon-bons, and the pigeons purr above them on the wire.

Nina winces at the screams of the teenagers scrambling back up the beach. She looks up, alarmed. As if she's just hurt someone. She looks for the bird. The gull. The damage.

Behind the last gangly teen is a fishing line, and on the end of the fishing line is a dead or nearly dead seagull. The boy's green cap covers most of his face but Nina can tell he's proud. She can see it in his bloated chest, his whoops, his laugh. One of the boys is filming it, as if the dirty deed isn't just enough to witness first hand. As if they need to relive the violence. As if they need to spread it, share it, and hook others into their monstrous game.

Nina, the nosy parker, is wide-eyed, skewered to the action. Disgusted. Her banana chair feels burdened by the sudden weight of her. Behind the boys and the dragging bird, she sees Georgia running into shore, board under her arm. She watches her watch the boys play with the dying gull.

'Oi! Oi! Did you do that?' Georgia screams at them. 'Fucking scumbags. Take him off! I'm gonna report you pieces of shit!'

Nina winces at her daughter's abrasive voice. Her whole body stiffens. The teens laugh and run on.

Nina hates bad language. She shuts her eyes at Georgia's display of anger and wishes she was somewhere else. She watches Georgia try to run after them but they're too far gone, already running up the hill towards the caravan park.

'Mum! Did you see them? I'm gonna follow them. I'll find their parents. I'll call their school. I'll call the police. I'm gonna ruin them!'

'Let's just go home, please, Georgia.'

The two women drive home, Georgia squirming and frenzied, unable to change out of her wetsuit, unable to talk. She's a fizzing sparkler, a Molotov cocktail.

They pull up outside the house and the women eye each other warily.

'Georgia, you can't do anything about it. Kids will be kids, you know. There's no point getting angry about things you can't control.'

'Kids will be kids? If I don't do anything about it, that makes me as guilty as them! God, I don't know how you sleep at night ...'

Georgia rips out her board from the boot and throws it in the shed. She trips on her legrope as she storms back towards the house, swearing her head off. Nina can't help but laugh as she watches her daughter through the kitchen window. Her wet hair is stuck to her pink cheeks. Her pale feet flinch on the rubble. It's getting dark and the crows start to wail. Mozzies slip in through the open windows. And the house tries to withstand the Christmas beetles now bumping against the glass.

In between Georgia's huffs and expletives, Nina tells her a story about bird eggs, stealing, bird calling and Mr Mitchell, while she cuts up potatoes. She talks about that first day in the city when the Queen was there, in an attempt to calm her daughter down.

'And, Georgia, would you believe it, we won! We won that big bird calling competition up in the city. Us little country kids beat all the fancy kids by a mile!' She places the pot on the gas top to boil and then turns to face her daughter. 'See, there are quieter, gentler ways of changing things.'

Nina has always wondered whether her daughter is her own version of purgatory here on earth. Parenting her has always felt like an impossible test. A test perhaps she hasn't done very well at. There is always so much lost in translation. Two conflicting perspectives. Words that sting from both sides, thrown like grenades. So often they are worlds apart. And yet she often feels closer to her daughter than anyone else.

Georgia disappears up the hallway and runs a bath. Perhaps the hot water will diffuse her napalm insides. She peels her wetty off and some of the weight of the last half hour dissipates into the hot suds. She picks up her phone and hammers out a Facebook status, describing every teen right down to their last detail. Even the green cap gets its own blurb. She posts it. She calls the local police. She reads her status to them. She wonders where else she can put it. She wonders how far she can spread this information.

She sinks down into the inadequate depths of the bathtub. She listens to the porcelain shimmer and creak under the water and to the quiet pop of bubbles that float around her.

In the next room, she can hear her dad has the news on.

… And in a dramatic turn of events, WikiLeaks founder Julian Assange has walked into the Ecuadorian embassy and asked for asylum, citing the UN declaration of human rights …

Georgia shuts her eyes and tries to relax. The frogs at the dam. They are so loud. The crickets outside the window. They are so loud. *But not bad loud. It's all good loud.* And every now and then she hears the *boo-book* of an owl. What her mum calls the old mopoke. She turns the hot tap on again and watches the water trickle in. When she returns to her phone, she sees nobody has liked her post. Nobody has responded. She doesn't even know if anyone has read it. Her words have floated out into the ether and joined all the other waste drifting around space, never to be seen again. There's just infinite space junk out there – swirling, tumbling words, spiralling around in some meaningless orbit. *Will that space junk ever collide with anything? And will anyone even care if it does?*

She bends her thumbs so they make a diamond around her mouth, like she'd seen her mum do so many years ago. She blows. Nothing. She tries again. Nothing. She repositions and tries again. Still nothing. But still, she repositions and blows, desperate. Her head turns to helium and floats up to the ceiling and bobs there. She cups her hands tighter and finally a raspy, blowy sound escapes. She feels her dizzy head re-join her neck and she hoots 'til the water turns frigid and her hands turn to kelp.

Georgia wraps her body in a towel like a little egg. As she walks through the kitchen, her mum can see she's been crying.

"Sorry, mum. It's just ... nothing scares me more than apathy."

Nina nods. She keeps nodding as she stirs her simmering pots, feeling the steam open the pores on her face. The sounds of the cooking almost drown out the frogs on the dam and the crickets in the bush. Almost. Nina watches the word *apathy* float around through the steam, like a ghost.

"My little thrush is in my pot plant again, about to have babies, Georgia," Nina calls out to her daughter.

But Georgia doesn't hear her. She is transfixed out on the veranda. Her hands cupped around her mouth. Swaddled in her bath towel. That novice bird caller has found her real connection, coming from several scattered spots in the bush. Mopokes and human together, *boo-book, boo-book, boo-book*. Making no sense and all the sense, all at once. And to Georgia that moment of union feels completely opposite, completely alien to the typed words from earlier that she'd spewed out into the ether.

Brooch

A pregnant woman walks down Merimbola Street, alone. Her eyes are fixed on the metal bird sculpture that beckons from the entrance of Panboola Wetlands. Her hands are fumbling, twisting, writhing into themselves. Her frown is casting ugly shadows across her forehead and cheeks. She fidgets. Her mind is a scratched CD, repeating, repeating.

As she takes an early detour just before the bridge, the saltmarsh becomes squidgy underneath her feet. The outsides of her boots are caked with mud, but her footwear is the least of her worries. She has an event looming that makes her tremble. It brings back bad memories, memories she's tried so hard to forget. But that day doesn't fade from her mind. It hurts every time she breathes in.

When she reaches the first face of the wetland, she sees, today, it is nothing but an antique mirror with moss growing in at the sides. It's forcing her to look at herself. The person staring back – well, she's never seen anything more hideous. Swollen, panicky, her chin with no definition; grief and trauma have done wicked things to her. She shouldn't be here wandering. She shouldn't be allowed to grow another human. She should be locked up, hidden. She is not fit for human consumption. Perhaps she never was. A swan disturbs the water like a spoon trailing through whipped cream. The woman's face fractures and her self-centred wallowing ripples out with it. There are bigger and better things happening here than her. Thank god.

She trundles over the wooden bridge, towards the old racecourse, in the hopes of seeing baby birds. It's spring and it's that time, time for babes to be born. She leans into the reedy edges of the wetland, her feet sinking lower, and she spots a mother and baby swamphen. The pregnant woman's crinkled face softens and she happily tunes into their universe instead of her own. The mother swamphen guides her baby around the footpaths and over on to a clear patch of grass. Can you see their feathers rise and fall and flicker as the cars on the road *whoosh* past?

Baby bird jumps over the shoots of grass; they are too tall for her legs and she often stumbles. But no matter how big the stumble she always picks herself back up again. She grows in confidence with every leap, and she chuckles as she lands and leaps again. The sun on her sooty black fluff feels nice and her mum thinks she's amazing, she can tell. Can she get higher? Maybe if she bends low before the jump she'll go higher. Can you see her little fluffy head bobbing through the kikuyu?

A car slows to watch the baby bird hop through the green. The driver grins, forgetting his life for just a second. Whenever the baby bobs too near to the road the mother herds her back in. *That's danger, baby, that's danger.* If you listen really closely, you can hear the faint *click clicking* of the mother's tail flags, flicking up and down. The two of them have grazed for hours in the early light as the dragonflies zoom overhead. The sun is creeping up, up now like a vine across the ceiling.

A larger supermarket has gone up over the road. Sprung up like Paterson's Curse. Big trucks are speeding in and past and around and often not watching where they're going. An echidna was killed here just last week. There does seem to be something quite personal about the roadkill these days.

Mother bird notices a woman with a round belly staggering over on the wooden bridge, watching her slowly coming closer to where they peck. *Is she a threat? Is there a baby in that pouch?* Her tail starts flicking, quicker and quicker, as the woman edges nearer. *Not this one*, she decides. The woman slows to a stop and stares. Then, as if in pain, continues ambling along the bridge and off towards the marshes.

Baby swamphen leaps and dances and weaves in and out of the grasses … *Watch me mum, watch me!* Mother bird smiles and continues pulling grass and chewing. Mother bird, like all mothers before her, is trying to come to terms with the reality of having her own beating heart on her outside. Her own soul bared, energetic, flouncing in and out of the grass and the world, outside of her safe ribcage. How much does a mother sacrifice? And yet, somehow, it doesn't seem wrong. It's just hard finding peace. *It's so hard to find peace.* Watch the mother now, deep in thought, a stroke of grass dangling from her beak.

A beep, beeping begins, steadily growing louder. *Beep.   Beep. Beep.   Beep.   Beep. Beep. Beep, beep, beep* … Baby bird, excited by the hubbub and wanting to get a better look at the huge road monster, springs onto the road. *Beep, beep*, she squeaks, *beep, beep*. She leaps towards the big rubber wheel of the supermarket delivery truck. *Beep, beep!* She screeches, laughing and leaping.

Mother is tired and has fallen deep into thoughts … *What if I cannot find enough food in this drought? What if the wetlands dry up completely? What if baby doesn't ever put on weight?*

Beep, beep, beep …

Mother bird stands up straight. She whips herself around to face the road. *Where is …? Stop, Baby! Stop!* Mother bird screams as she leans forward and throws herself towards the wheel. She uses her wing to knock baby back towards the grass; she uses every bit of strength she didn't even know she had. She sees her baby jump, jump, through the grass, exhilarated ... *Beep, beep, beep, beep* ... and the big road monster takes off again, blowing big black clouds behind it. Puff, puff. And it's gone.

Baby jumps.   Jumps.   She stops and looks back. She watches her mum's feathers move in the road's breezes. *Whoosh, whoosh.* Another truck flies by, *whoosh.* She giggles as her mum's feathers blow up, this way and that way, in the wind.

Baby bird is only a week or two old, one driver decides, as he slows down and peers over his window. The car stops. The driver gets out and walks over to the stationary mother bird half flattened on the road. One of her legs is sticking up in the air. The man watches the fluffy little one eye him cautiously. He's not dressed for this kind of thing, he thinks, looking down at his navy work suit. He looks back at the baby bird shaking in the grass. With open arms he tries to shoo her over towards the water, away from the road. *Ya. Ya. Ya,* he commands in an authoritative voice. *Why today? Why'd it all have to become so personal? Today, of all days. It's presentation day today,* he thinks, and shakes his head. He doesn't want to look back at the dead bird so he keeps his head down as he dashes back to his car. This isn't his problem; he didn't do it. *That's life,* he tells himself. Gotta keep going. *I'm late, I'm late, I'm late,* he tells himself over and over again all the way to work, as if he's on a loop.

The baby keeps running in the same direction through the uneven grass blades, tripping, slipping, swerving. She nears the saltmarsh but she misses her mum. She isn't to go anywhere alone – she remembers mum's lessons. She crouches near a log and waits until the humans are absent. *Humans are peculiar beasts,* baby bird thinks. She just wants to be with her mum.

She darts back towards her mother as soon as she can see a clear route. Other cars and road monsters begin to pull over. Baby bird scampers through the tall grass straight towards the road. Her own little tail flags have started *click, clicking*. How strange it feels! Her own body telling her things when her mum's isn't. Baby bird's hard feet hit the black road and she sees those familiar feathers straight away. It's like her mum is spreading her feathers further and further in the wind, like she's dancing.

Little baby bird uses her beak to nudge her mum's head. *Come on, Mum. Come on!* The humans come at her now, arms outstretched. She is scared. *What's going on? Mum? Why aren't you moving? Quick, Mum …* The humans come closer, almost touching her now. Some clammy hands grab her around her middle and she goes up, up, up into the sky, towards the water. Away from her mum. *Muuuuum!*

Over on the water she can see all the other birds like her there. She can see the whole wetlands from this height. It is crazy big, too big … water that goes on and on with birds of all different colours and shapes bobbing, paddling, feeding. All she'd ever known or thought of was her mother and the things that were right in front of her or whizzing by. That was her world. And now she can see that she is part of something much bigger, much scarier, but also spectacular.

With caution and gentleness she is placed under some rushes, her feet deep in peat. *It's cold for spring,* another human thinks, as he watches the orphan fumble through the red marsh weed. *Much too cold for babies, at least.*

The walking human with the big belly from earlier comes trundling back towards baby bird. The woman looks sad, almost like she's crying. *Is she crying?* Baby bird wades around looking up at her, remembering her from before, from before when her mum was here, and it was just them and everything was normal. She watches her warily through the reeds. *Is she danger?* She listens for her mum's tail flags to flick but there's just the moving water at her feet. She notices her own tail flags flicking again, ever so gently and quietly, like a whisper. They are faint but they are all she's got, so she tries to strengthen them. She tries to find her own sounds in this new world. She tries to listen to her own body even though the sounds are faint.

Look at the little thing hiding in the shadows. Can you see her little fluffy body hiding there in the marshes?

The woman snails along the wooden bridge. Step.   Step. Step. She stops and stands, hands on her middle and watches the baby bird closely. From behind her, a wild bunch of black cockies erupt in *araarrk, araaarrrkkss* and the woman is startled. She drops her phone on the ground as the cacophony of gossiping cockatoos burst out from the trees and then spring up into the air. Everyone turns to look at them. They ripple and soar as if they are one barking machine, all charged up. The noisy birds shoot up and out like a flying black arrow. Out of the leaves they shoot, from the branch of the biggest gum, straggly and matte green, leaves flipping in the wind – there it goes. The arrow is released loudly but smoothly and it sails through the day, puncturing any other story. They all flap together. Can you see their wings synchronised?

The human woman turns back to the orphan baby and there are others there now. Little sooty fluffballs of birds bob around in the ankle-deep water. It is a meeting of the miniatures. All paddling. All fine. The woman relaxes. It's much harder to connect to a group than it is to one. The guilt of what she is subsides and the balls of fluff all start looking the same. They paddle off with parents and the woman breathes deeper, her shoulders sink lower. Not one bird is left by itself, treading water. The orphaned baby is not left alone – she has friends, a home. Almost as if the woman doesn't trust it, she longs to dip a ladle in the water and dollop a bit of the soup in to a bowl to examine it closer, find that little babe. But no bird has been left down there alone. She can't deny it. She can see it for herself.

Viewing herself now in the antique mirror somewhat differently, she wonders whether fear is all for nothing. Perhaps beauty, like everything else in life, just needs to be contextualised. Perhaps her body, with all the blizzards it's housed and healed from, is the most beautiful thing in the world. She crouches with difficulty by the edge of the old mirror and stares closer at her face. If she looks fear in the eye, it can't run, it can't ulcerate, or multiply. But it can change shape. It can soften. Perhaps, it can even sparkle if the sun hits it right.

The woman stands up straighter and breathes easier, the pain in her pelvis momentarily numbed. She struggles down to the ground to pick up her phone and she notices the screen is smashed. But it doesn't worry her. The road ahead of her feels somewhat sunnier. She leans over to grab a sprig of blossom from a nearby tree. She twirls it in her fingers like a wand and then keeps walking.

She turns and crosses the road. Windswept feathers tumble like acrobats across the bitumen and she looks for her, the mother. Where is she? Then she spots her, vibrant but flush, like an ornate brooch. The melted bitumen has become ormolu in the sun, royal gold fringed. The blue and black feathers are silky in the glare. The red of her beak like a wee gemstone. Can you see her fixed there as if she's nothing but decoration? A mark of what was and is. You can see she was beautiful, and there's a peace to her that comes from somewhere else.

And as if in a narrative, the woman pins the metaphorical brooch onto her blouse. At first it pricks her, *ouch!* And then she just surrenders to the weight of it on her chest, as it rises and falls, rises and falls, and the rhythm of it carries her all the way home.

Empire (Part One)

No sound so empty as the pound of that drum,
nor one as infectious or trite;
some loved its cold grip, they succumbed and rose,
with rumours and English gold to the throes of what's next,
what's next, was the call.

Waves moaned to the sand defeated and spent;
ghosts whorled in the spit of mad men.

He sits puffed with a head full of air. Only to separate.
Whose emulsion is he?
There he goes, that great head levitating, higher and higher!

    But, through the flurry of ducks and harpooned whales,
    he falls to an end no-one knows.
    The oil, untraceable. The water returns to the sea.

'The Beat of Arthur Blair', Charles Spin

The black wings of the duck ruffle in the silent spaces, pushing the debris away. The duck dives. It flaps above the water, looking towards the mountain that stands above it all, Balawan. The morning breaks like a seed pod above the horizon. Golden rays spill over. Babies stir and suckle and water splashes and drips from the duck's wings like paint across a canvas.

Twofold Bay, just south of Pambula, is still as a lake, and birds' voices pour along the shoreline. The stench of rotting cattle and whale meat wrecks the vista and there is not a pocket of air free of it. But the stench only burns now for visitors. Locals have acclimatised to the pungency and the colossal abattoir that has become their town. Shelters and gunyahs stand in clusters around the bay and sea mist drifts over the roofs. Women are not forgotten by the day. Their hair, oiled, braided and plaited, curls along the pillows and grass mats. Wooden houses stand like soldiers in the street. Some men lay in their underwear, clutching harpoons, covered in whale blubber and blood. They are still tossing from the fight. Stubble lines their jaws and their bedrooms smell of sweat and sea. Other men lie in their gunyahs, lined with foliage and propped up with steel. Many are caught in limbo, between sea and boat.

Spirits from long ago rest peacefully in the waters, gentle in the blue grass, soft on the shoreline. They've seen the man they call Blair sketching plans, marching with purpose, talking a lot. Even the ghosts can feel the air of change simmering within the town. They watch. They dart like quicksilver from crevice to crevice. Even the chrysalises buried in the dirt can feel the rumble of his feet as he walks. About halfway around the scalloped Twofold Bay sits a large clearing, with what is beginning to be known as Blairtown. The small inlet boasts milky sands and still sea and if you don't look too closely, it all looks quite amazing. But can you see him? Can you see Arthur Blair sitting there in his dining room, eating fresh bread and butter? You can tell he is not expecting visitors, but there are guests about to arrive. The room is long and wooden with golden trim. It's almost as if Blair can feel you watching him — he twitches and there's something in the way his eyes move. You can see he's all done up in his sea attire. There is a lamp in the corner that throws out a ruddy glow. Though it is mid-morning, the lamp remains on. A large bogong moth flicks and flaps on the windowsill. Powder rises from its wings and floats through the sun's rays like dust, tiny planets in a celestial haze. It seems to have been injured by the clasp on the window. One of its wings is a little torn. If only it could just get outside where it could spread them and try to fly. Blair's eyes flit towards the moth. He tightens his fist around his butter knife. His mouth shortens. He stands and struts towards it. Watch how his butter knife flattens the wings and the powder floats upwards. He holds it down. Flattens it in seconds. And in its sudden deadness, its tiny legs quiver a little under the knife. Blair watches closely until each leg loses its fight and he returns to his table.

Outside, Blair's new slaves guard his fields and livestock and carry marble slabs across the lawn. Before Blair, there was no such thing here as slavery. Can you see the white men standing on the edge of the precipice, howling orders? They wear stifling uniforms that seal in their sweat like jars of anchovies. And Blair pays for that cased-in sweat. He pays big. But only to his men. Blair's slaves get small morsels of bread and a change of clothes. Not much, really. They often try to escape, so Blair watches them like a hawk. He pats his belly at the table. Anyway, this money is on loan, you see. Aye, the sweet promise of an empire. He burps his whiskey into the morning air and the sour smell lingers around the table.

He watches the men toil through the window, sweating in the sweltry sun, and he lashes more creamy butter onto his bread.

'More!' he roars from the dining room.

Several women can be seen fluffing around the kitchen, sifting flour, cutting large hunks of raw meat and stirring a bevy of pots.

One woman rushes bread out to him as if he will starve there on the chair.

There are three guests now standing at Blair's entrance. They intermittently screw their noses up at the smell of dead whale carcass. Bits of blubber wobble along the shore and whalers hack at bodies with knives. It's a bloodbath, aye, that's for sure, and one of the strangers on the doorstep mumbles to nobody in particular. The mumbling man appears almost crazed, thumping a drum that swings from his chest, *Dum-da-dum-da-dum* ... He's freshly shaven and conservatively dressed in vest and tie. Over one shoulder is a bag of what looks to be books. Bulging. As he stands there, he seems confronted. As if a cold chill has come over him and rippled up his back. He is distracted. Shakes his head.

Another man is very drunk. Stains over his front. He is all moustache, that one. It wavers like a black skirt over his taut lips. His little bush-girl wife is trying to coax him away from the entrance and back on his horse.

'You've had enough. Christ, Harry, you've had enough!'

He doesn't seem to hear her.

The third man is all rugged up in a large buttoned jacket and appears rigid and blunt, like a hammer. He's all moustache too and sports a dark, finely groomed beard. Binoculars hang limply from his neck, as if he's here to whale watch. This man strides up to the doorknocker and gives it a good *rat-tat-tat-tat-tat.*

Blair sniffs the air like a collie as a woman rushes to open the door. He strains his neck to get a geezer at the party. Can you see the other women eye him from the kitchen, waiting for direction?

The three men stand at the entrance. The woman outside, Betty, yells curses to one of them. She carries a copy of *The Bulletin* in one hand and she lugs a soiled rope in the other. She leads a Clydesdale away from the house. Her head is sunken, her gait long. There are babes attached to her, sleeping soundly.

The man with the drum keeps striking it, *dum-da-dum-da-dum-da-dum* …

'Cheerio, cheerio, lads,' Blair yells from his chair, then turns to his maid. 'Hurry on then, get that horse and woman off the lawn. I'm not having horse shit over my property.'

Cold air whips in through the door and freshens the mood. Blair has sat in the one position too long and has pins and needles up one side … watch him lean from side to side and shake his legs.

'You come here together?' he demands, pointing his finger at them like a hook. His brow dances. His eyes travel down, up, down, taking in every detail. It is with much vigour the men shake their heads and talk over each other, explaining their very accidental meeting. The meat has started roasting in the oven, each chunk rubbed with fresh rosemary. Gravy is being ladled and the steam whorls upwards from the bowls. The smells are almost too much for the visitors and even the horse outside starts pawing the ground.

The men wander in, introducing themselves. Joey is the seaworthy, whale-watchy one, Charles is the clean shaven one with the drum and bag and the drunkard is 'Harry', with a spirited burp. Despite Joey's pulled back tongue and raging consonants, Blair cannot decipher his accent, but decides this fellow must be some sort of secret agent here to spy on him and check how he's using all the money. *His eyes have seen some seas,* Blair observes. You can tell a sea man because the eyes are always deep like a vat and they glisten like beetles. All that glare for all those years, you see. Blair smirks. *He knows the sea, aye, he knows the sea.*

Blair places his hands on the ground next to his feet, stretching his hamstrings, and he surprises himself with how flexible he really is. Despite his satisfaction he maintains a watchful eye on the visitors. He doesn't like their spontaneity, their timing, and least of all their large intellects. He sees how the big, fancy words curl off their lips like it's no big thing. But he refuses to be intimidated, not by these dreamers. He only half-listens to them and he doesn't wait for them to stop talking before he begins.

'And what with the drum, chum?' Blair turns to the man with the drum and bag.

'Aye, I've bought you a humble snare drum, Mr Blair, to signal big things. I heard wind of your plans and I've come to write about your new empire. You see, Mr Blair, I'd like to write a suite of poems about vision, and yours has piqued my interest.' Charles throws his boy-like hand out towards Blair as if they are equals and Blair eyes it like a rodent.

There is no hand shake and instead Blair turns and begins a series of calf raises. 'I see. I see, lads. Worthy intentions, Charles. Mmm, I see.'

Blair straightens up and looks them one by one in the eye. Is this meeting significant? Will his legend and legacy be celebrated by these men through their arts? They haven't really offended his ego so far. Watch how Blair paces the room in front of them, shaking his head, staring, pacing. But his heart's unsteady and the alarm bells start to sound; Blair trusts no-one. They can stay for lunch but no longer. They have no real purpose here, except maybe Charles. He seems to have the right intentions. Ahead of his time, that one ... despite his boy-like appearance.

Another bogong moth appears next to the body of the dead one. It seems to be inspecting the corpse. Blair has not yet seen it. Can you see the moth find its mate? It's a grim scene indeed.

As the human-size clock chimes in the corner it becomes clear as to why Harry is here; he heads straight for the whiskey. He clambers up on the table like a loaded dog on all fours, defiant and howling. Blair has seen this poverty before. He watches Harry snatch at the crystal, and the golden liquid spills and splodges over the polished wood. This vile weakness is what happens to poor men. His nose crinkles as he thinks of poor men always waiting for their billies to boil.

From his sock, Charles pulls out some parchment and a quill. He tips his book bag onto the table and out tumbles parrot feathers and books of Yeats, George Eliot, Henry Lawson, and Joseph Conrad. The feathers float through the air and settle about the place. Straight away women come running to clean them up.

'Grab him ink! Ink!' cries Blair.

The women run from the table to the kitchen with several elaborate quills and ink pots and stuffing the strewn feathers into their apron pockets. Charles begins scribbling immediately onto the pad. Furiously. Like he must be done before the clock's last *dong*. Watch him race, scrawling like a mad man. The energy catches like a sneeze around the room and the men become spirited. You can see Charles glance around, through the window, to the chandelier, to Blair, and occasionally back to his drum. He's in his own world now – the gold-dusted diorama of a poet, where even the drabbest fleck can be polished.

Blair stands amidst the chaos, unperturbed, chest bloated like a buoy and lectures as if profound. 'Look around you, men. Soon these walls will be all gold, this will be the capital of Australia and I shall be its king. It'll be grand! And don't fret, I've built a lighthouse. Aye, she's the jewel, a grand one indeed.' Blair gloats like a fat rat in a trough, stroking his long sideburns with his index fingers. The men raise their eyebrows.

'Aye, a lighthouse, indeed,' Joey and Charles chime. Harry does not seem to have heard and continues slurping away at the table, staring out the window.

Joey has seen the greedy glint that glimmers in Blair's eyes before. He has seen it in men's eyes at various ports abroad. The greed for gold and silver is what he had written about during his travels. Hell, he even harboured his own precious metal lusts. *Gold tastes good in any language, through any means*, he thinks to himself. He paces over to the elaborate window pane and stares out into the field. He flinches at the sound of the whip's crack against skin.

'Aye, whatever you've got to do. My heart grows dark to say, but you've got to make yer money spread.'

Blair smiles, 'Aye, Joey, aye. All I see here is profit and progress, I tell you, profit and progress.'

Harry now slumps against the wall, reciting a saddened verse from the poem, *Faces in the Street*. Something about the level of the windows and God. Blair's always been a Patterson man himself, he ruminates. Who wants to hear about hardship and toil when you can have a rollicking good time? He stops listening to Harry and feels quite giddy with control. Charles tries to tune himself out from the chaos. He's scribbling quicker than he ever has now and the pages keep turning over. *Profit and progress*, Charles writes, *profit and progress*. He wonders whether his poem is becoming a parody instead. As the scene unfolds and the words fall out of him onto the parchment, he starts to see it is not the piece he had originally intended. When he stood on the doorstep, he had a bad feeling. He couldn't shake it. Now he lets it shape his words. Time itself seems a farce. He feels the beat of Blair's ego throbbing in his peripheries. The throb of it swells every word from his quill. He is meticulous with his proofing, but as he goes, he finds there is nothing paradoxical about this. It is loaded with much more than vision, humour and dreams. Perhaps it's even a cautionary tale. He wonders where it will end, and all he can envision are some brittle bones, undiscovered, and the hollow sound of a drum pounding in an empty room.

Around their conversation, the building is growing in size. Slaves and workers are tapping, hammering, cowering under the shrieks of Blair's men. Some are defiant. Some are trying to escape. Some are marching inland under close surveillance. The walls are rising. The gold fringes are glistening in the midday sun. Big bullocks are heaving materials up the hill. The fireplaces that started with chimneys, solid bricked squares are now being finished with gold inlay. Ships are docking on the shore and workers are carting materials in by the bundles. Trees are crashing to the ground. *Whomp.* Long, rusty saws hang tethered from the trees' bowels. Possums flee across the ground. Stray gunshots leave puffs of powder in the air. Fat cows are staring down the barrels. Nails sprinkle like confetti over the concrete. Big sandstone slabs are being lifted from ship to building site. Blairtown is springing up, growing, bloating, glistening, and pennies are falling from the sky and green sterling in the thousands, burning as it hits the turf.

On the outskirts, Betty stands with her husband's Clydesdale and another housemaid. You can hear them talking over *profit and progress*, about children and rivers and mountains, about births and deaths and isolation ... and men. Betty is writing with a quill on parchment against the horse's hide. Infants run around them, squealing and leaping. You can see the two women laughing as they brush down the horse. Behind them is the sinking tangerine sun.

Balawan is shrouded in night, kissing the clouds. There are grey wisps of ghosts floating over the water's edge and rooftops. It's almost black night now, and you can hear the town's women whisper to each other, to the night sky. The hundreds of whispers sound like cicadas clicking and whistling away in the dark. The wind has calmed and the spinifex on the shore is swishing in the breeze. You can see some women wading home through the river. They carry wisdom like jugs upon their heads. Can you see the eels writhing through the weed around their feet? The women do not flinch. The horizon is heavy with night and black clouds sag upon the ocean peaks as if playing a game. The world is gathering above the site. The clouds churn. A man called Blair is examining a bogong moth fluttering underneath the weight of his butter knife. He pushes the knife down. Down, again, until fluttering stops and the bogong lovers lie still, a powdery explosion of what was and is on the golden windowsill. Darkness is building. Workers retire for the day. Spits of rain pepper their faces. The whispering fades out to complete silence.

The sun's arms reach above the horizon. They grab the edges of the clouds and they slowly pull their body up, up until it throbs like a bloody heart above the sea. Another day. As the ships return, ducks fly across the shoreline. Their black wings smooth in the wind, their eyes focused. They do not flutter anymore, they soar. They do not dive, but rise. They leave stories that echo around the land, from peak to peak, rock to rock, along rivers, winds and sands. Stories that light the sky and quench the thirst. Stories that hold us in their weave.

And just like Charles wrote, *he falls to an end nobody knows. The oil, untraceable. The water returns to the sea.* That empire was never finished. Arthur Blair became bankrupt and ruined and then vanished like a thief into night.

And that old drum, can you see it? There in the middle of that long table? It still pounds in the many hearts of men. Can you hear it, in the empty spaces between profit and progress?

There, hear it?

Dum-da-dum-da-dum …

By now, the ghosts have almost drifted away in the southerlies. And that empty tower that never became a lighthouse still stands there, waiting for purpose. If you ever go there, stare up at those five fateful letters — **B L A I R** — and let the ego of it drip down into your eyes like mud.

Pulse and a Tusk

The old Nissan Pulsar putt-putts along the Princes Highway. The muffler hangs precariously low and barks like it's got croup and her father has his foot flat on the accelerator pedal.

'Where are we going?'

The tinkly seven-year-old's voice strains against the muffler's cough. Anyone can hear Georgia is hopeful like a hobby horse. She knows it's a Saturday and all the kids at school raaaave about Saturdays. The desperation glitters around her milk-stained mouth as her eyes wish and wish and wish for spangly things. Or even just a song.

'To Eden, darl ... to Norm's ... he's just very isolated, you know—'

The mother, Nina, stops abruptly like an emu on a cliff edge. Her feet dance there for a while, trying to find the right words.

Nina met Norm one day in the supermarket. She watched his brittle hands fail to hold his groceries. They were like rusted claws. Plop went the rice. Plop went the tea bag box. He was a busted zipper drawing the aisle to a close. She helped him to the cash register and she continues to help him now, eight months on. She couldn't watch those shelves eat him whole again. She would hold them back 'til the zipper separated from its track.

Georgia will just have to understand, Nina thinks. She looks out the window and takes a breath. She speaks cautiously, her voice not the salve it once was.

'I promise it won't be for too long, George ...'

Georgia angrily flicks through her baby animal book now like it's trash, throws it on the floor, and then kicks the back of her dad's seat. Georgia is all claustrophobic, thinking of Norm's dark living room – the stuffy, dusty nooks and the plastic pill dispensers open and empty like old advent calendars. She can smell the place already. Her visual mind pictures the cricketer in his baggy green and whites poised in front of the TV, probably a cheap figurine from a lucky dip a long time ago. It is with a more favourable disposition that she visualises the taxidermied flame robin that sits on a twig in a glass dome by the side window. Georgia isn't allowed to touch that one. She doesn't know why. It's so pretty.

There's nothing she can do about her destiny. She has watched her parents help many lonely folk out through the years, like bakers tending to their loaves, trying to build their own special gold-plated gates into heaven. Or perhaps it was the guilt that made them do it. Perhaps her whole family was born melting, dripping with that Catholic guilt like hot tar onto a road. She wondered whether every decision for the rest of her life would drip, drip, drip with that same hot sting. She wondered whether they enjoyed it. They looked and sounded like they did. She knew she didn't.

She has brought no other toys with her to play with. If they'd warned her, would she have picked up a toy nicely and walked out the door? No way. Full cataclysmic tantrums. Screaming 'til she rippled. She understood why they didn't tell her things, but that didn't mean it was the right thing to do. Again, she'll be forced to invent narratives with those six hard little elephants of Norm's. She can see it now – her on the floor, saving the herd from measles or a raging mammoth while Norm's favourite daytime television shows with beautiful people all talking garbage blares at a thousand decibels. She grunts and pulls her jacket toggles down and the hood shrinks and shrinks, and tightens at the back of her neck like a pannikin.

'But you can play with those elephants you love?'

Georgia sinks into her booster seat like a submarine and disappears down into the deepest sea. She only barely notices the cows outside in the paddocks, all facing the same way, whiz past. It is such a long drive down to Norm's. She does love those elephants, but there are only so many hours one can journey across the dusty carpet with the six of them and still find new material. What do her parents take her for? Her shoulder bag of creative dust is growing scant. At the end of the day they are still just carved little elephants, with baby-tooth tusks, that sit on a mantelpiece. They are like ancient marbles that won't even roll.

Norm doesn't talk much, and his loneliness emanates from him like a wandering pulse. Anyone not solid, not grounded, could have their own heartbeat interrupted by this huge Norm-esque pulse. If he could walk better, Georgia believes Norm would follow her and the elephants around the room, trying to fight off the mammoths. He has that look about him; desperate for connection but unable to do it. She can always feel Norm watching her when she's playing with the elephants. But she doesn't know how to include him. She guesses there is life in him, but it's buried like a seed and nobody waters it. She doesn't know how to water it.

Sometimes when she looks at Norm, he looks like he's dead. Still, not breathing. Slumped over like his head is melting into his heart. She's only seven but she wonders what this black creature is that burrows down near her middle, its limbs slowly unfurling around her frame. It does not feel child friendly. Like a dollop of black ink that drops onto blotting paper, it bleeds out. She tries to ignore it.

Her mum is animated in the kitchen, organizing the tea bags and spices into glass cannisters. Her dad is reading the local newspaper to Norm, but Georgia can tell he can't really hear anything cause his eyes are blank like stones. The gas heater in the corner sounds like a cow and the room is too hot. She knows her cheeks are pink.

She crawls over the carpet like a wolverine, slick, stealth, to the empty electrical point on the side wall. She flicks the switch off and on. *Flick. Flick. Flick.* She just does it to see the red dot on the second flick. She can feel the danger of the red through her fingers. *Could she electrocute herself by doing this? How does electricity work?* she wonders as she stares vacantly at the flame robin in the glass dome over under the window.

Norm humpfs and it makes her jump. But he's not looking at her. She turns towards the fireplace looking at the elephants. She goes over and strokes the smooth marble of the biggest one. Her little cupcake hands ferret around to the head and her fingers thrum the white ivory tusks. Those bright satin pegs with the pointiest of pointy ends.

Norm stands, slow and bent. He angles towards the hallway and then begins his shuffle. Navy slippers at the forefront, edging, edging closer to the end of his frayed rope. Georgia watches him go, fading into darkness up the hallway.

She holds the biggest elephant up and pushes the polished face in so that its sharp ivory prods her cheek. It's good to feel something so barb-like and pronged. The juxtaposition of the textures occupies her thoughts for a while and the *bom boms* fade into whispers. *Tusks are excellent,* she thinks. *Such a shame humans don't have tusks next to their noses. They'd look so much more interesting.* She could get those boys at school back. Really tell them to tusk off when they called her mean things.

Her father and mother say things to her as they pass but she ignores them. She watches her father limp around behind the vacuum cleaner, room to room. He pulled a muscle in the hospital bed race at the Pambula Mardi Gras on the weekend and she thinks back to the moment they won, her dad and all the other Yowaka River men sprinting up the main street and winning by a head. Her head. She was their weightless 'patient', holding on desperately as they flew through the town on an old hospital bed. Even though she is weird and has a bit of a weird life, she knows now what it feels like to fly.

She grabs the other five elephants off the mantelpiece and lines them up on the curly carpet. She's invented pastimes for them. Names. Narratives. Whole histories that each one carries with it. She plans their next adventure. It starts at the fireplace and it traverses the odd nooks and trenches of the living room, and then meanders down the steps and into the back sunroom. They must make the great annual migration to find magical jungle leaves that will help them live forever. They might meet companions along the way. It will be treacherous, but it will be worth it. The elephants have read about these jungle leaves in the papers. Oh yes, these elephants read the newspapers every day ... she giggles and nods at the thought, and then briefly feels herself grow even weirder, involuntarily pushing the walls between her and any other child and possible friend higher. Ever higher.

There comes a sound from the bathroom. A loud one and then another. It is all tings and gasps and clatters. Her parents rush to the noise and it's all emergency, emergency. Her mother gets on the phone and her father yells to her from the bathroom. That and the *bom boms* echo through Georgia's ribcage once again and bounce around in there, almost aggressively this time, like plastic balls in a ping pong machine. *Ping, ping, ping.*

She won't move now from where she sits and her Weet-Bix from this morning's breakfast sits spikily in her chest. Other adults arrive, saying words she doesn't understand. There were sirens when they arrived and there are no sirens now. When you spend so much time with older people, there's often these moments ... the mortal ones that weigh a thousand pounds and kink ever so easily.

She looks at the mouth of the flame robin, slightly ajar as if he's saying something, but she can't hear it because of the glass cylinder around him. She wonders what a flame robin sounds like. She wonders whether the moss and leaves around him are real. Is he even real?

She speeds up her mob of elephants, but instead of going forwards they feel the need to circle. Round and round her ruminating position, galloping with their cumbrous bodies and ancient hearts. Their bodies want to wave their white flag, but their tusks burn the flagpole. They're in a trench and there are cobras all around. They are spattered with venom. She can feel their spittle and zaps. The house twitches with adrenalin.

With thunderous stampede the herd tramples all the cold-blooded beasts and skewers them with their tusks. The serpents are punctured, flattened, deadskis. And eventually Georgia feels the house settle and she wonders whether she has any parents left. Did anyone remember her? Her anger fizzles out and her mouth is dry, plain-flour dry.

All these people in navy uniforms shuffle around in the sunlight at the door, angling a long metal contraption every which way. Georgia catches brief glimpses of it all but she doesn't look for long.

Finally, she grabs the elephants and flies them through the stale loungeroom air towards the sunroom. The battered beasts indulge in the paradisal tastes of the jungle leaves. Just the needed elixir. We all want to live forever, don't we? She sits a moment and wonders whether people do really want to live forever. But if we lived forever, would anything actually ever feel good? She looks around her and the people have all disappeared. The air aches. The room feels godless and the sun winks at her through the dirty windows.

She is interrupted by her mother, who croaks now from the hallway. She appears, wretched, on the flipped over doormat. She looks like a giant egg that has cracked, good and proper.

'Georgia, Georgia, there you are. We're going now ... put the elephants back where you found them.'

Georgia stands the elephants up, stoic, defiant on the mantelpiece. She stands back. She knows this time is different, she can feel it right down to her Apple Pie shoes. The pulse that usually bounces around the insides of each room fades. With every passing second, she starts to realise that what remains of the *boms* is no longer around her but actually inside of her and she can hear nothing else. As if she's caught it from the air, as if it's hanging around, contagious; Norm's own Black Death. She's infected. Can other people hear it?

The car rumbles to life outside, the muffler barely just hanging in there.

Beep!

'Georgiaaaaa!' Her dad yells above the horn blast.

Her eyes study the herd above the fireplace. Resilience shines on them like dust underneath the halogen. And even though she was never allowed to play with the robin, she knows they had a relationship all the same. They understood each other. He was delicate, breakable. His bright orange chest was only that bright because of the glass. In real life, something that perfect is sure to fade, surely. Her grubby human hands would have damaged those feathers. She loved him; she knew that. And maybe one day she'd hear him really sing, out of the glass, out in the open air. She closes the living room door and something sets in her, like concrete in a mould.

'Georgia! Hurry up! Get in the car.'

As Georgia walks out into the open, fresh air, she grows up … kind of like she's taking off a jumper or something. Instant relief from a temporary ill. Like it is nothing and yet everything at the same time.

A year trickles by in a Year 1-coloured egg timer. Georgia tramps in from school, weary. Sport day always takes the mickey out of her. She's not skilled in outdoor pursuits and there's not one ounce of competitive vigour in her. Team sports are the worst because she has become comfortable with personal loss, but she is far from comfortable with causing others to lose … that hot tar drips heavy and hot over her. Pesky teacher made her go goalie … she wanted that position like wrangled metal in her bed.

Today is all barnacles. Her stomach is clogged, her heart cuffed. Her whopping big backpack falls onto her bedroom floor like a leaden brace and she dumps herself in her chair, crabby as a brooding chook. A loser boy from the high school, who lives in the bush up back, threw rocks at the back of her legs all the way home from the bus stop. That dirt road of hers was much, much too long when you were being pelted with rocks. He would yell, 'Connie Wacker, licks her dackers …' but she didn't know what a Connie Wacker was. It sounded like a type of shell or sea creature. Maybe tomorrow afternoon she would run … She thought she would walk to make her seem brave but now she thought about it, it just made her seem stupid. If she ran it would be harder for him to get a good aim. She could be fast when she really needed to be.

Feeling better now she has a plan, she sits down. On her desk is a lunchbox-sized parcel that is covered in anger and sticky tape. It has her parents' names on it, but it is for her. She can just make out the word D A U G H T E R scrawled across it in messy handwriting, as if the parcel is shrieking at her. She plucks her plastic scissors out of her top drawer and tries to make her way into the parcel, at first gingerly, then savagely as the plastic proves thick and tricky to break.

Inside is a black felt bag. On the bag is a note.

Norm Straw's last will and testament states:
Nina and Warren's daughter (Georgia) gets elephants.
Signed (with an illegible old-person scribble)

Georgia can't read all the words. But she recognises Norm, her parent's names, Georgia, daughter and elephants. She sprawls the contents across her desk as if someone's going to take it all from her. The six elephants clonk around the wood and she stares at them. Her plasticine fingers snatch at them and hold them into her chest, letting the smoothest smooth in the world cool down her unrest.

They're all here. Six beautiful soldiers. But something is different. There are holes near their trunks. Brutal wounds, gaping. They've been disfigured. It is all bloodless and deep. Where have their tusks gone? Not even a flick of white remains. She feels like her spine has been pulled out of its own skin cage.

She runs to her parents, messily.

'Mum! Daddddd! This, this ...'

She pushes them into her parents' chests, disgusted.

Her mum holds one of them up to the light, its gash darker than its body. Nina studies the holes, twists the body around, her eyes transfixed in the wound ... it's an adult-sized kaleidoscope.

Georgia wonders what evils must tessellate in there. Her parents are confused and start spouting among themselves in adult whispers she's not meant to hear. Georgia recognises terms like *pathetic, greedy*. New words like *ivory* slither through the room sucking out the air.

Georgia surmises that Norm's family has done this ... Norm's family, from up in the big city, who never seemed to give a hoot about Norm, never visited him. The filthy lot of them couldn't even hand over these little critters without ripping out this thing called *ivory*. Those tusks were the size of damn Tic Tacs. She shudders just thinking about the flame robin. The glass shatters in her mind and all of his feathers turn grey and dusty; the world pilfers what it can from the tiny creature.

Everything seems nonsensical. Georgia hurts, not just for the elephants but also for Norm. He left his magical herd for her, even though she was never that good to him. She sees now that Norm had a family of slaughterers. Icky, faceless crims. She wishes she could go back through time and cuddle that old man. Maybe their lonely pulses would have dissolved ... maybe he could have lived longer, and she could have prevented this.

The hot tar drips until it hardens. She flings her tears from her face onto the floor, leaves her bickering parents and stamps back to her room. She splits like wood under an axe in the corner of her room until she kicks her wall. It doesn't dint but she has time. She lines them up, her army against the world. The gaping holes in their face making them look fiercer by the second until she's almost scared of them.

Her passiveness now fettered, her ire churning like butter in vats, she stands towards them, legs quivering. She will never let this go, like the lonely pulse, the *bom boms* that follow her around like a beat. Like a strong hold that fires each step and lights each ravine, she has an army behind her and she won't rest. Each day she rakes and scavenges, typing into the void, always hunting for a magical elixir that might cure the world from its dirty greed.

And every now and then she thinks she hears it, the song of the flame robin coming to her in the distance.

Neighbours

Wollongong, the city of steel and sea. Such industry. So many countless hours of study. So many stories of migration, refuge and survival. Some told. Some untold.

At first I didn't like it; the carbon floated through the air and landed on my windowsill like pepper … always made me think I'd get cancer. But then the balminess and the ducky, pondy university grabbed hold of me, shook me and told me to wake the hell up. It offered me a second chance. Second chances are important.

That's why I'm telling you this story.

It hadn't been long since we moved into our 1970s two-bedroom brick unit in North Gong. It was old, sure, but I loved how comfortable I felt there. I loved how close I was to the beach. I loved the free bus. That period of my life was special … just my husband and I in a two-bedroom unit, cooking stir-fries, learning about literature, going to the beach and watching re-runs of Ellen.

We shared a veranda with our neighbours and at first this had scared me. My home was my private sanctuary. I'm an introvert and I struggle having visitors. I struggle especially with 'pop-ins'. You see, I don't have any boundaries and sometimes I find it hard to see where you end and I begin. It can get pretty messy sometimes, so I have to work hard to protect and know my mind.

I can't compromise. It's not nastiness, it's my own form of survival. If you've not lived my life, then it might be hard to understand ...

My shift had been extended. The uni was busy with O-Week and what not. My legs throbbed and I hadn't eaten since breakfast, forgotten my lunch again. I would never complain because my year of begging for work had not left me. My 60th job rejection in the mail that both my parents saw had not left me. Neither had all the hours of applying, pretending that all these miscellaneous jobs – bathroom maintenance, waitress, receptionist, gardener, parking inspector, you know, the list went on, were my dream jobs. Absolute dreeeam jobs. That's what I said. But, as seen in the many, many rejection letters sent to my parents' house, they knew as well as I did that I was not the most suitable. I was a qualified teacher, but teachers all seem to move to the coast and there was a surplus of them ... and I think a year is enough time to wait for a relief teaching block, don't you? *Be a teacher*, they said, *there'll be heaps of work. You're so suited to it.* Well, there wasn't and I wasn't.

So I moved to Wollongong and went back to uni, good on me. And I got a job at the uni, good on me. I was so excited to have a job again, I bought myself a new pair of boots and they were fancy looking but not the most comfortable. I didn't care. I looked the part and that was vital, because I never ever wanted to be without a job again. And on this one day in particular, I had to stand in the same spot for about eight and a half hours and I'd walked to the bus stop and I'd walked back from the bus stop and my boots made my back hurt so I was in a bit of pain and as I headed up over our driveway and down into our little cul-de-sac I could hear the excruciating sounds of moving furniture. I looked up and saw my husband and the guy that lives across the road struggling to lift an awful-looking washing machine up the front staircase.

*Please don't move next door. Please **don't** move next door,* is what went racing through my mind. Then I heard a voice, a woman's voice, talking in Arabic. All frantic and emotional; she looked a bit knackered, if I'm honest. She needed a good sleep. Her head scarf was a little torn on one side and hanging limply down onto her shoulders. Two children were standing either side of her. There was a teeny boy, maybe seven or eight years old, with a shaved head. And on the other side an equally teeny girl, maybe nine or ten. She was shy, I could tell ... and her face was exceedingly twinkly. There were just so many stars in it. I accidentally smiled at her and she gave me one back. I think it was the stars that made me do it.

The boy was about to explode, busting for me to talk to him.

'Hullo, hullo, hullo, hullo, hullo ...' he repeated at me.

'Hullo,' I responded. I didn't want to. I didn't want to make friends because that would mean they might not understand that I didn't want any friends, that I had important boundaries that must be upheld. They might think I was free as a bird to chat and entertain and stuff around. I was not. I was busy. I was studying, I was working, I was writing, I was reading, I was watching Ellen.

The little boy was joyful, zipping up and down the driveway, treading on my toes, singing in Arabic. Kids do this funny thing to me – I don't want to talk to them but my mouth just speaks anyhow. Like my inner child is always wanting to run with them but my mind is so cumbersome and heavy it tries to jam it in a cage.

'What's your name?' I said, motioning with my hands.

'Aalam, Aalam, Aalam, Aalam ...' he yelled as he ran back and forth across my toes and the incline of the driveway. He said it so fast all the letters merged into each other and I couldn't separate them. His shoes were old sandals that didn't quite fit. His big toe hung over the edge.

'Ah … lum?' I repeated to make sure I got it right.

'Aalam, Aalam, Aalam …' he shouted as if I got it wrong. Maybe I had … I still didn't know.

As I looked at the little girl, I asked her the same question and the mum was now yelling at her in Arabic. But she wasn't angry-yelling, more stressed-yelling. The little girl looked back at me and in the quietest, most articulate voice, said, 'Sabori.'

'Sabori,' I repeated.

She twinkled again and went back to calming her mum. Her shoes were Velcro runners that were faded to the point where I wasn't sure if they had been pink or purple.

The mum was babbling at me and then at her daughter, her hands moving at alarming speeds. I assumed she knew no English.

Sabori watched her mother, nodding. Then she turned to me and asked for my name.

She tried to repeat my name back to her mum but the mum just shook her head.

'Can you speak English?' I asked Sabori.

She shook her head and indicated with her hand that she knew a little.

'Mum, no speak.' Then she pointed at her chest and said, 'Learning.'

I was tired and my feet hurt so I just waved at them and walked inside, hoping to not have to go through that again.

A couple of afternoons later, I got home later than my husband. I was held up at work again and I had gotten into trouble during my shift because I talked for too long to a client who was having a bad day. I was upset. I just wanted to please bosses, not disappoint them, but as the woman spoke about her awful day, I found myself wanting to cry with her. I found it hard to distinguish between her day and mine. Between her sadness and my own. It was a lot to take on.

As I reached the driveway, I could hear Aalam's voice, loud, energetic, at a pitch my head couldn't deal with. I could see his little round tummy underneath his too-tight shirt. He had climbed over the metal fence and was sitting on our veranda telling stories to my husband in very broken English. My husband was laughing. As I climbed the stairs, I thought, *if he starts telling them to me, I will just explode.* I just wanted a bath. And silence. And as I opened the door and walked inside, my husband turned and waved to me, and Aalam didn't draw breath. He just kept going with his story, his hands waving everywhere. I've never heard anyone talk that quickly … it was a lot of energy to walk into. As I walked into the bathroom, I could see him showing my husband how his little sandals were breaking.

'Look … broken,' he said and pulled the sole open. He laughed as he looked inside the sole.

I poured myself a bath and got in. I pulled my stupid cheap boots off my feet and threw them in the corner. As my skin hit the heat, my eyes started to leak. I hated being yelled at. I'd done the right thing talking to that client for a longer amount of time, hadn't I? She was crying and lonely and stressed. She needed someone to listen to her and wasn't that my job? Customer service was so confusing. Here was the customer and the service they needed was for me to listen; if that wasn't my job then whose was it?

I sunk under the water and in my head I started my escape route; I pretended I was famous and on the Ellen show, getting interviewed about all my made-up achievements. I was telling her a funny story and she was laughing.

When I popped up, I could hear my husband had come inside our house to fill up his glass and Aalam had followed him.

'You should cut all your hair ... chop, chop!'

'Cut all my hair off?' my husband asked.

'Yah, chop off. And grow big beard. Like my hair. My hair is cut. Like me. You, chop, like me. And because you are man, you grow big beard.'

My husband chuckled as he filled his glass up from the tap. I couldn't believe there was a small child in my house yapping, like Aalam was yapping, after I'd had such a shitty day. I tried to block it all out.

'Mr Ash, why your hair so long?'

Then the mother knocked and yelled at Aalam through our door.

'I go now. But you, you cut hair, Mr Ash.'

As he disappeared, I could just hear him start up his usual song.

My husband had really enjoyed the interchange, I could tell from his chuckles. I just cried into the water.

I know I sound a bit pathetic here but please keep listening. I want to tell you this story.

A few weeks later, the girl, Sabori, came running along our veranda looking for Aalam. Through the side door, she asked in perfect English whether I'd seen her brother. I hadn't. I could hear her mother shrieking from her unit. Her voice shook. *Aalam! Aalam!*

I was in my pyjamas and I was mid-sentence with some prose poetry but I told her he'd probably just be at the clotheslines telling someone a story. I often saw him there. Searching for connection. Wanting someone new to listen.

Sabori and I ran down the steps, down the next ones, through the courtyard and around the back of all the buildings to the corner of the yard where all the clotheslines were. I could hear his voice already, though I could not see him through all the hanging bedding.

'... the best singer in the world. I tell you, Miss Mavis, I tell you I am.'

'Well, go on, let's hear it then,' Mavis said with a smirk.

Mavis lived above us and had never said a word to me since we moved in. She smoked a lot and had a cat. She wore the same tartan pants every day of her life. I liked her more with each day that passed. We understood each other, you know.

Then Aalam started to sing in Arabic a tune I'd never heard him sing before. He'd learnt a new song! Praise be! The last one was doing my head in ...

He sung for about 20 seconds and it ended strangely, as if he forgot the rest of the words. His little voice could hit several notes at once and was not a voice I would have described as a good voice, but there was something about his eagerness that was endearing. He sung with gusto and volume and a joy that was rare these days. Made me miss teaching a bit, I guess, if I'm honest.

After the song faded out, he bowed. Long and low as if he'd just delivered a speech to the United Nations Council. Then Mavis clapped and hooted like an owl.

Sabori and I just stood and watched him. I knew she was livid at him, but I admired her in that moment because although she was so mad, she still just waited patiently for him to finish singing. Mavis was laughing and I'd never seen her smile before. Her front teeth were golden and some glistened as if they just might be real gold.

Sabori gently went to Aalam and talked to him in Arabic. She politely excused herself for interrupting Mavis and then took Aalam by the hand back to their unit. I followed behind, just admiring Sabori. I'd been so excited by the singing and by seeing Mavis laugh and speak that I'd quite forgotten that I was wearing pyjamas and it was almost midday. Truth be told, I thought Mavis was mute for at least a year.

A month later, I came home from work and was desperate for a drink. My shift had been big and I'd stayed up all the night before doing an essay. I'd worked all day off three hours' sleep and I needed some respite. I struggled up the stairs, kicked off my cheap boots that were now falling apart, and poured myself a pear cider. By this stage I had stopped sitting on my veranda for fear of being caught with Aalam. I now sat in the spare bedroom so he couldn't see me through the side window. I sat down and swigged at my chilled cider, looking at my squashed white feet. I started to reflect on all the interactions I'd had that day ... was I good at my job? I hoped so. Was I improving? I hoped so. Then there was a knock at the door. It was soft and short. Not like an Aalam knock. I tiptoed out and over to the door and looked through the peephole. I could see no-one. I tiptoed back and as I went, they knocked again. Soft and short. I went back. I opened the door and there was Sabori with a pile of letters.

'Sorry, sorry, but mother says you need to read these to me. Our lights won't go on.'

I sighed. Then their door opened and her mother's face looked out at me and said, 'Good?'

I said 'good' back and they both came in. This was the mother's first time inside my house and I was embarrassed. My house was hideously messy due to my late-night study session. There were papers everywhere. About 15 books were lying open, with Post-its all over them and they were spread over my treadmill and lounge. The mother looked around excited, wanting to see in my kitchen, in my laundry, in all the rooms. She ran in and out of them like a child. Her robe and headscarf were all the one colour on that day. She was wearing sandals. They were old. Her feet had walked a lot in them, I could tell. The skin was brittle and cracked. She stopped and took off her shoes and left them by the treadmill. She started moving the uni books that I had positioned over my treadmill and my embarrassment burned; why hadn't I cleaned my house that morning? Why was there no comfortable place to sit? What an absolute grub I was.

'I'm so sorry about the state of things ... I've been ... studying,' I said.

Sabori chattered to her mother and her mother responded. It felt like they were saying many, many things, but when Sabori spoke in English again, very few words were spoken.

'Mother said she loves your house.'

Sabori put extra emphasis on the *loves*. I assumed she must be lying so I would read her mail, but the mother did look strangely excited, and she kept looking at the treadmill where she had cleared my books for me.

Again, there was a lot of Arabic going down. I felt like an outsider in my own home.

'Mother asks if she can have a go on ... this,' and Sabori pointed to the treadmill. At this I laughed, because the mother was not dressed for it at all. But what was I supposed to say? I looked at her long tresses of robes and I scooped them up with my hands.

'Yes ... but I'll have to hold these up.'

The mother jumped onto the treadmill with the agility of a

child and I pressed the start button and increased the setting until she was walking at a moderate pace. She giggled. Sabori giggled. They chatted amongst themselves as she walked triumphant and I could see now where Sabori had got her twinkles from. I stood holding the entrails of jade green robes to my chest and marvelled at how random my day had become. I was hankering for some more cider but I just tried to hold it together.

The mother bounced off the treadmill after a few minutes and Sabori thanked me and her mother bowed and they both laughed together like best friends. Then they sat on the treadmill ledge, because there was nowhere else to sit, and I knew my role then was to read.

… I cleared my throat and *(reader, thank you for letting me tell you this story)* as I read the letter to Sabori, she talked at astonishing speed to her mother. The mother remained silent. The speed at which she wove between two completely different languages was to me incomprehensible. She had only been in the country for two months and already spoke English better than most people. Turned out, their electricity had been cut off because they had not paid their bills. I told this to Sabori and she told me they had a lady who came to help them do these things but she hadn't been for a while. Apparently, she was coming tomorrow. I got up and walked over to the miscellaneous drawer my husband and I called the 'shit drawer', and pulled out two candles and a box of matches. I gave them to Sabori and told her to use them very carefully and to blow them out before they went to bed. Then I said the 'lady' could help them pay the bills tomorrow. I didn't know who this 'lady' was or whether she was really coming tomorrow.

The other mail was junk mail and then at the bottom of the pile was a small sized envelope from Iraq. I could not read the writing on this one. Sabori took it back off me, surprised, and handed it quickly to her mother. Her mother ripped it open, shards of paper went everywhere. She read it at a great speed. Then she looked up, her eyes wet, said something to Sabori, bowed her head quickly to me and then ran out the door. Sabori hurried to read the letter as well. Her eyes darting from one side to the other. Then she looked up at me, confused. Wondering whether to tell me.

'Is everything OK, Sabori?'

She said the letter was from her father's mother. It said they had still not found their father's body. 'He was killed,' she added ... like it was no big thing, just business as usual. 'It is war over there, Miss Georgia. We ran. Got things and ran. Mother said to come, and we ran with her.'

Her and Aalam had never talked to me of *before*. I wondered, then, just how many stories her mother had burning inside her, aching to get out. How many stories I would have loved to hear if only she spoke English or I spoke Arabic and, of course, if I had more time. I wondered whether Sabori would one day tell those stories, or whether by then she would be so scarred by the stories that they would have frozen inside her like stalactites. And even if she wanted to break those cold daggers off and offer them to someone, there would be nobody to take them. Nobody that would want to listen to anything so hard.

'I'm sorry, Sabori.' I didn't know what else to say.

Sabori folded the letter up and slipped it back into the envelope.

'Thank you,' she said and quietly scurried out the door.

I plodded back into the spare room and sat on my office chair.

I gazed blankly out my window as the bubbles in my cider glass slowly disappeared.

The next week Aalam came running onto our veranda. I'd stopped caring by then about the cleanliness of my house or my car or the state of my appearance around my neighbours. I felt like we'd passed the niceties and were now into the natural, comfortable, family-like state of living.

'Mr Ash, Mr Ash,' he called to my husband, 'We need car, take us to pray. Please, please. Lady not come. Please?'

My husband agreed, put on a shirt and slipped on some thongs. Aalam laughed at his thongs.

'Funny shoes, Mr Ash.'

His little joyous face bent over to look at them closer. He touched the Billabong logo and tried to sound out the word, 'Bee-bee-bee.' As he sounded out the strange word, he stood up to take in my husband's whole frame. As he got to my husband's head, his face screwed into a frown.

'Mr Ash, no, no, why you not cut hair?'

'Um, Aalam, I guess … I forgot?'

Aalam looked seriously at my husband's hair and pulled the curls out 'til they were straight on one side. He felt my husband's chin with his tiny hand. His eyes lit up. My husband had forgotten to shave that day.

'Ooh, yes, Mr Ash, you grow tiny, tiny beard!"

My husband laughed and patted Aalam on the head, 'Come on buddy, let's go.'

Sabori and Aalam's English was improving every day and our conversations were growing fuller, deeper. Despite us both being teachers, we were continually amazed at how quickly the children could learn and adapt and navigate such strange, new spaces. And I was worried. Aalam had really come to love my husband, and him, Aalam.

Please don't relax, I need to tell you this story. It is of the greatest importance.

So, my husband took Sabori, her mother and Aalam to the nearby mosque to worship and I started to cook vegetable stir-fry. I put more spices in than normal because I was growing more and more jealous of the delicious smells that would drift in from next door. No matter what I put in the stir-fries they never smelt as good as next door's. The mother often offered us to cook us dinner but I felt like it was a line I didn't want to cross, even though my stomach did. I watched re-runs of Ellen while I cooked. *Be kind to one another*, she said at the end of each episode. I loved how simple that slogan was and yet how tricky it often was in practice.

When my husband got home, I was sitting on the couch eating stir-fry and watching the TV screen. He came and sat in front of me with some scissors and asked me to cut his hair very short.

'And why might I ask have you all of a sudden decided to cut off your locks?' I said, somewhat perplexed.

He shrugged.

'How short are we going?'

'Pretty short.'

He sniffed and shuffled around the floor in front of me, distracted.

I nodded and started to snip. We both stared into the TV, and it was the episode where Ellen was talking to Malala Yousafzai. I found myself transfixed by Malala's face. The way it remained calm despite where she was. Her gentleness. The way her face was skewed on one side from when she got shot by the Taliban. There was something unnaturally placid about her expressions for someone so young. I was surprised by her ability to make jokes and laugh in the face of all that she had seen. If I was her and I sat next to Ellen, a white millionaire, I might not be so jovial. Malala's body had seen so much, survived so much and yet here it was on our television screens, changing the world.

Then my husband turned to me, out of the blue and said, 'Hey, do you like facial hair?'

And we both laughed.

I laughed at the randomness of the question. I laughed, until I realised he wasn't kidding.

The next week, I limped home from the bus stop because one of my shoes had finally broken while at work. The sole had almost completely torn off. It was funny, sure, I laughed with my colleagues ... but as I walked home, I couldn't help but feel embarrassed and full of self-pity.

Listen now, this is my favourite bit.

As I reached the top of our driveway, I could hear Aalam shrieking with joy. I could see him dancing and leaping around our veranda; little Aalam had 10 enormous white cockatoos perched around him, scattered over the ground. We often fed them seed and they were chewing and cracking old husks littered around the outdoor setting. I never thought much of them. I was used to birds. There were heaps where I'd come from. I always bought them seed, 'cause that's what my mum used to do. It was habit. I'd forgotten what one of those birds looked like from a child's eye.

Aalam was gleeful with the company and the afternoon sun shone down on him like those halos in the old renaissance frescoes. He looked like a little cherub.

'Miss Georgia, Miss Georgia, look, look, bird friends!' He waved his arms around and the large birds jumped around his feet and bounced along the coping. Excitement bubbled out of him in little involuntary yelps. And the way he'd said *friends* kind of tore me apart. Something inside of me recognised a lonely part in him too. *Yes, bird friends.* I smiled. And I thought of the bird friends I had had when I was younger. Those bird friends saved me from many darknesses.

When I got inside, I retrieved our box of seed from the cupboard and went out onto our veranda and stood next to Aalam. I kicked off my stupid shoes that I didn't even think looked good anymore. In fact, they'd almost started to look ugly and I vowed to never wear those broken pieces of shit again.

We were both barefooted now on the veranda tiles.

'Hold out your hand, Aalam,' I said gently.

I poured some seed into his palm; it shook as I poured.

'If you're very still and quiet, they might even jump up onto your hand.'

He was full of spark, that boy. His little hand was trembling and I thought the cocky mightn't risk it. I willed it to, so hard. If that bird wouldn't jump onto that little guy's hand I'd bloody grab it with my own hands and hold it there just so he could see it up close. Just so he could feel the connection. But I didn't need to worry. One of the birds, with its crackling beak chomping away on husks, slowly walked over to Aalam. The bird looked sideways at him, this way and that. I watched its powdered and cracked feet creep along the clanging coping and finally stretch one claw out onto his hand. Aalam looked at me as the bird came closer and he was really smiling. Not just normal Aalam smiling, but the biggest, busting smile I've probably ever seen. You know the type of smiling that even if you'd covered his mouth you could still see the smile in his eyes, in his cheeks, in his neck, in his ears, his skin, and chest. Nothing could hide a real smile. Aalam was silent and I just watched his face as the bird bowed down to eat the seed.

It was a pleasure that I never thought I'd feel at that late stage of the game. I felt like I was intruding on someone else's intimate moment. A moment perhaps only a mother should enjoy. Did I deserve to experience this? I didn't know but I also didn't move. I thought of his father momentarily. It was a hard thought that I couldn't entertain for too long.

I looked closely at Aalam's face staring so intensely at the big bird. I felt a flutter of what I know now to be love stir in me. I felt my eyes sog up and I didn't like it. I missed teaching. I missed watching children grow and learn. It was the greatest privilege there was. I stayed there with Aalam for about an hour, just watching and helping him feed those huge birds. They were almost as big as him and I'm sure if they really wanted to, they could've picked him up with their claws. But I wasn't going to let anything happen to Aalam. He'd be right, I was there. And I remember in that moment feeling enormous gratitude. Gratitude for just being there with Aalam as he fed the birds. I just sat there and did nothing but watch and laugh and pour more seed. I didn't pick up my phone. I didn't superglue my shoes. I didn't start cooking dinner. I just was there. And the TV was off.

A month later, Sabori came to us early in the morning. Knocking oh so quietly. My husband and I were massively hungover. I felt nauseous. I knew it was her knocking because nobody knocked that gently. Her mum was crying in their unit; we could hear her through the walls. When I looked through the peephole, I could see Sabori had tears in her eyes. I opened the door, my head spinning like a wheel.

'Miss Georgia, sorry, sorry, can you please just tell us who sent this? Do not read the rest of the letter, just the top. I can read the rest.'

She held a piece of paper in front of my face. Her little finger pressed along the letterhead where it said, *The Department of Immigration and Border Protection.* I noticed her finger shaking slightly next to the big black letters but I didn't think anything of it.

I was surprised Sabori asked for help reading because she had gotten so good at it. She was perhaps one of the cleverest children I had encountered. I saw her reading English novels on the veranda all the time. Novels, for crying out loud. If I was still teaching, she would have been my dream student.

'The letter is from The Department of Immigration and Border Protection,' I said blankly, vodka vomit from last night almost reaching my throat.

She nodded.

'And is that an Australian government thing? Can you explain who they are?' She looked worried; her long eyelashes blinked more than normal.

'Well, I guess they are in charge of saying who comes in and out of the country … I don't know, I'm not an expert, the government kind of bores me. Why, what are they saying? Want me to read the rest?'

She shook her head and took the letter back off me. 'So, they are real government people?'

'The realest,' I said, half asleep and definitely still drunk.

'Thank you, Miss Georgia.'

'Mmm-hm,' I nodded and wandered back to my bed, quickly forgetting the interaction had ever happened. I fell back asleep in seconds.

That was the last time I spoke to Sabori. In fact, my husband and I slept all through that day and into the night. We only got up to eat some takeaway that evening and we did hear furniture moving but we thought nothing of it.

And when I got back from work the following day, I walked down the driveway and Aalam was not jumping around the veranda. I could not hear his voice. There were no stories. I could not see his or Sabori's seats on the veranda. Nobody was there watching the world go by. I couldn't smell anything cooking. I couldn't hear the mother's impassioned voice rising and falling.

This, this is important now, keep listening.

There was no singing. No singing! And as I walked up those steps, their door was slightly ajar. I pushed it and looked in at the bare room.

Like the room, I was gutted. I went in and sat in the middle of their living room, feeling the full impact of who I was, and who I am, and I took off my new, much more comfortable shoes and cried.

And all these years later, I still feed the birds that come. Those *bird friends* of mine. And my husband still grows a full beard. Not because he's vain, not because he can't be bothered shaving, but because this is a very important story. And there's nothing more important than stories.

A Race to the Bottom

Georgia sits Baby on the kitchen rug and dumps a pile of seemingly safe utensils in front of him to play with. She's been busting to wee for an hour or so now, but every time she has tried to go he has needed something else. Once she's satisfied with the lack of danger she dashes, quicker than a slick to the toilet. She's Black Caviar. Mighty in her leaps and mighty in her precision, until her last sprint through the laundry towards the bathroom. So fast, too fast – she doesn't notice the heaped basket behind the first door.

Clatter. Failure all the way down. On her way down she hits her leg on a stool and her head on the side of the bathroom door. She is large like Black Caviar, so the fall is clumsy and weighty and causes as much damage as possible. A tower of folded clothes falls on top of her and her head shakes from the hit, spinning like she's Margarita-sloshed on a Friday night. The thought of drinking a Margarita again makes her weepy. It's been a long time since she's been able to clock off. Under the fallen clothes it's dark and she surrenders there.

It's the ear-splitting screams of her baby that tear her from her brief reverie. He's hurt himself, somehow. Her fall now a distant memory, she jumps up to standing, wash-towels and undies windmilling off her in every direction. She leaps over her first hurdle and she clears the clothes easily. She veers around the corner and can see Baby writhing, purple-face screaming on the rug. She picks him up, frantically checking him for cuts, bruises or harm. The ways a small person can hurt or kill themselves seem infinite. There is no end to this bumbling, crying risk factor. It's a love that is so beyond her control she finds it extremely hard to sleep at night, even though she's dog tired.

His purpleness fades to a softer rouge and the damage is not apparent. He is holding tongs, so perhaps they poked him in the eye. Perhaps he hit his head on the drawer. Could he have concussion? She searches his eyes for changes in the pupils. He's wriggling and screaming too much to see properly. She sits on the toilet, uncomfortably, while Baby bites and hits her. Going to the toilet is like completing a Bronze Medallion these days. With her free hand, she starts googling concussion symptoms on her phone. Her search history is full of teething remedies, chopping baby flesh with nail cutters, baby not sleeping, baby poo that looks like rabbit poo and dying from no sleep. Turns out you *can* die from no sleep. These tedious searches whittle away her days and nights. The baby continues to cry, and they are real tears. She doesn't notice the drops of blood on the floor around her. She doesn't recognise herself anymore, or her house, or the 'menial' activities that fill her day now. The ennui and fatigue have rendered her, well, a fair bit bonkers.

She flushes, washes, and paces, rocking, always rocking. It's a soft Simon and Garfunkel song she hums to him now. Her stress is vibrating through her skin onto his and she's aware of it. Hopefully *Scarborough Fair* will calm them both. She just makes up the lyrics.

The baby's crying fades and he starts grabbing at her face. His fingernails are sharp and she swears he breaks skin, like little blades in surgery. She says, *no, no, that hurts me*, but he continues. He likes her being reactive. It isn't until she sees the red on his fingers that she freaks out. Where is the blood coming from? Is it him? Has he knocked himself somewhere? Then she sees the red out of her left eye and she feels her face and finds more blood there. With one hand she holds his arms down, and clutches him like a float, searching for the mirror. Perhaps it is the strange blood on her that scares him.

The face is red. The face is strange, like someone she knew a long time ago. There's a gash on the side of her head from her epic fall. She doesn't care, as long as it isn't the baby ... nothing some wet wipes can't fix. Biodegradable wet wipes – how did she ever live without them? She cleans her face up with one hand while tightly holding the baby. Perhaps she fell because she hasn't eaten. She can't remember the last time she ate. Her food is never cooked anymore, never nutritious, never mindful. She doesn't have time. It's like any self-care, really, it just has to slip in hurriedly where it can, or not at all.

With his razor-sharp fingernailed hands, the baby tries hard to help wipe her face. She thanks him for being so kind, while grimacing with pain. Georgia tries to make a mnemonic peg, but she knows her tired brain will forget almost instantly; cut his nails later when he's asleep. One. Bun. She imagines a fingernail in the bun. She imagines eating a fingernail bun and it makes her feel sad. In the hours she spent feeding the baby last night she had felt delirious and alone and she stared at her husband's back, trying to imagine being a baby ant and having to climb over that back to see to the other side. Every skin follicle, every silky hair, every bodily bump, a giant climb for the little ant's legs. She feels instantly sad again because she has a weird mind.

Georgia has a few minutes to get to her monthly book club with the girls, and she hates being late. She's a bit dizzy and she should probably go to the doctors but she's too tired for anything else right now. She has to get to her one nice thing she does a month. She didn't expect motherhood to make her feel this walled in, this lonely, this anxious, this desperate for connection. Since giving birth it had felt like someone had kicked her beaten body into another galaxy and she could almost see her ravaged frame there, hunched and hurting in the middle of nowhere.

She looks in the mirror again and notices a huge scratch mark right across her right cheek from Baby's fingernails. No matter. She's got on her favourite flower shirt and her green sunnies and she feels upbeat, she's still got pizazz. She's heard people talk about each baby ageing your DNA by 11 years. *11 years!* She remembered hearing this before she'd had her son and she laughed. She thinks of it now and the blueness under her eyes doesn't seem even a little bit funny. The scabs that won't heal on her hands don't feel funny either. The cold-sore blistering and weeping on her bottom lip is deadpan serious.

She helps Baby scramble over the clothing and out to the kitchen. She doesn't want to upset him again, so instead of taking his suit off (he hates getting dressed in the cold) she puts another clean one over the top. She straps him into the pram, grabs her bag that is full of every possible item Baby might need and walks out the front door.

It's sunny for winter and the air is almost warm on her skin. There is life outside – the smells of coffee roasting sweep across the road and dogs are being walked up ahead. Her struggle for survival feels polarising next to this bubbly vibe. A woman walks by with her coffee billowing steam in a beautiful marbled pottery Keep Cup and Georgia marvels at how ethical her little town has become. There is some hope in her shadows, sparkling little rays of it that she catches in cupfuls. Another mnemonic peg. Two. Shoe. Now jam the shoe into that lovely pottery cup. She starts feeling sad again because she knows she doesn't have a spare $35 lying around for such a pretty coffee cup. She misses having her own income. There was something vitally reassuring in that independence. But her gut tells her that Baby needs her right now. And she has to listen to it. Then she remembers a fingernail in a bun. Then she remembers the scratch on her face and how tired she is. But she picks herself up because she's going to book club! She's got friends and they've also got babies and they are going to have a stimulating grown-up time talking about politics, the climate crisis, and have ethical debates about consumerism and this book they've hopefully all read ... Ah, just to be around adults and to use her brain again!

She nears the café and she can see them all filing in, in their neat, clean and very sensible attire. They each look like they are high functioning adults, ready to conquer. She shouldn't have worn her flower shirt or her green sunnies. She should have resisted the gold shoes. She privately winces at her own stupidity. She's the old mare in the stable, how dare she think she's a shiny racehorse. Her chest tightens when she remembers how tired she is. How will she function if they ask her a question? Long gone are her tea drinking days. All she drinks now is coffee, and if she wasn't breastfeeding she would inject it.

She walks in to the café and finds herself a seat. Nervously. She feels their eyes all over her and Baby. First, she thinks they are judging her and she is failing. Second, she thinks they feel sorry for her with their little half-smiles. One, bun, fingernail burger. And the gavel falls. Two, shoe, crammed in a coffee cup. And now she wants to cry. She sits and slides her sunnies up onto her head, making her feel instantly naked. Her eyes are literal windows into her fatigue. Her head flinches so nobody can stare into the windows too long. She starts talking uncontrollably because she doesn't know what else to do because if there was silence right now, she'd break down. She stares into all of their pretty faces and she thinks she can see what they're thinking. They've all decided she's not coping very well. It's in her tizzy hair, her untidiness, the dried blood they can see on her hand. They can see it in the baby's undone hair sticking straight up and out to the side, they can see it all over the dirty pram, in her messy handbag, all over her tired, eye-bagged face, they can hear it in her incessant talking. Or maybe the tiredness has made her paranoid? Is she just being paranoid?

She draws a breath. 'So, how are *you* guys going?' Her child is trying to backflip out of her hold and knock all the table condiments over. The sound is calamitous, and Georgia tries to ignore the whole cafe worth of faces glaring at her.

'Me? Oh, I'm fine. Everything is good,' one responds.

'Yeah, no news here,' one adds and gives her daughter a spoon to play with.

Their children play happily on their laps, quietly cooing and smiling at the right moments.

'We're really good, thanks.'

The last one is smug, and Georgia feels it's all a personal attack. She asks them how their babies are sleeping.

'Sleeping? Oh, yeah, great.' It's the last one again. And then she sticks her reply in like a knife. 'She sleeps all night.'

Georgia feels the deep hole inside her filling with tired, uncried tears and her skin crawling with anxiety. Insecurities rise and pop around her, but she's determined to try harder. She wants this connection. She scours her jumbled mind and pulls out what she believes to be her most interesting thoughts and concerns about Adani and coal, current energy trends around the world and, of course, renewables, about the impact this warming and its ramifications will have on this next generation. She lets herself get angry.

'And what will we tell our kids when they are old enough to understand — stop touching everything, no, don't touch that — as to why we didn't do more to stop this?'

She has to stop the sentence there because her baby is screaming to be put down. She gives in to stop the piercing sound and puts him on the ground. As she leans over, she can feel the throbbing pain in her breasts from surplus milk and she knows there is no way in hell she can feed when she's this stressed. She scatters a few grubby toys around the floor next to Baby. He ignores the toys and crawls towards the front door. Wanting to escape. Why can't he bloody just sit still like the others? Perhaps she will never finish a sentence for the rest of her life and all these unfinished sentences will just tangle into themselves, and when she dies and they dissect her brain for science that's what they'll find – a mass of angry fishing lines, a big silvery knot of sinkers and hooks and frustration in a ball on the sand. 'Yep, it was the unfinished thoughts and sentences that killed her,' the scientist will declare.

Georgia can feel her face burning and her whole body heat up with her son's unbridled attempts at freedom. Reluctantly, she gets up and walks over to him, anxious in case she misses someone responding to her questions. Her mind is dancing in fast-forward, over and over. Is she being weird? She feels so messy inside she isn't sure of anything. If only she could just finish a sentence or hear someone else finish a sentence. If only she could just grab a full sip of her coffee …

Everyone is holding their babies like beautiful handbags and chatting about blenders when she returns with her baby. It's all so civilised. It feels cold, brutal, gladiator-like inside her chest. She's wanting adult connection but she's squeezing the sponge too tightly – they are all running from her. Her paranoia is now gnawing into her wrist bones. She can feel its teeth sinking into the marrow. She looks into one of their cups and their coffee is gone. They drank the whole cup! She takes a big swig of hers and Baby tries to knock it out of her hand. It spills all over her arm and him and it doesn't matter because it's completely cold now. And the pains in her chest from all that goddamn milk are nearing mastitis level and she definitely can't handle that beast again.

She sits and tries to listen. They talk in full sentences about the plot. Full sentences! Georgia can hear their sentences come to an end, but she can't compute them. Her baby wriggles out and down onto the floor again under the table. All she wants is to join the conversation. She has so much to say about this book. Everyone can see her baby now to the side of the table kicking his shoes off and putting them in his mouth.

'Don't do that, Baby, not in your mouth.'

And he crawls back under the table away from her with the dirtiest part of the shoe in his mouth. The others begin their discussion again but she's under the cafe table, bum in the air, telling her baby not to put the shoes in his mouth. She tries to force them back on his feet but he's kicking too hard. She eventually sits up at the table once more. So what if he eats his seedy shoes? She tries to catch up but by now she's so out of the conversation, she's the old mare again that should surrender and lie down in shame.

'I thought the twist at the end was effective. I mean, I really didn't see that coming …'

'I thought it was totally predictable! I could have told you what was going to happen about two chapters in!'

Then the tablecloth starts pulling and a saltshaker disappears off the edge and clamours to the ground. Georgia grabs it before everything goes over the edge. Conversation stops while Georgia dives under to grab her destructive human and the women all patiently hold the tablecloth while she sorts it. She imagines one of them running the heel of their shoe into her back leg while she's down there, making them all decide she's gone lame. *Two, shoe, coffee cup, take it and run before you're euthanised*, Georgia pleads to herself. As she creaks to a stand, baby in one arm, she doesn't want to make eye contact in case they see her tears wobble over the lenses. She clings on to her baby like he's her only friend in the world, she kisses him on the cheek and buries her nose into the fat folds of his neck. She excuses herself, and exits the café feeling like the last of her species. Whatever species that might be.

She stumbles back home, dragging her beaten frame with its garish decorations. Her sunnies are completely fogged, and her eyes drain like punctured bags. The street is a muddy racecourse and she's breached the discourse and is giving the finger to the officials. In front of her is the pram. Her baby tweets from his sheepskin nest, plumping up his plume. Her hands hold the pram handle too tight, like a torch in front of her. The dark suffocating tunnel of a sunny street of people is all around them.

Just before the gate to her house a man stops her and says some nothing remark about Baby. He is older, 50 … 60 maybe?

'… Isn't he a beauty?'

She nods. Smiles. *Yes, he is, thank you,* or something like that is what she says.

'And another one on the way I see ...' he adds, patting his own tummy and looking down at hers.

She shakes her head. She didn't know she could feel worse than she already did. This was becoming a weekly ritual. People in the street asking her if she was knocked up again. Asking her when the next one was due. *Time for another,* they'd say, when she was trying to buy her bread or post her letters.

She wondered who her body belonged to. What was her body? Was it a conversation starter? Was it a weapon? An artefact? A baby factory? It felt like a weapon to her. A weapon people used against her.

She leaves the man still staring at her, smiling. She blankly clicks the gate open and pushes the pram towards the door like a sad sword. Whatever this battle was, it wasn't just about her. Wasn't just about today.

As Baby and her walk through the front gate, he reaches up with his little sticky, salt-encrusted hands for a wet, open-mouth kiss. She can feel his body relax now. Back safely inside, she feeds him and feels the relief as her chest empties. Then she puts her baby on the floor with his op shop trucks and he takes to them. Of course he wants to play quietly with them now. She walks to the window and stares out at the god-awful butterflies nonchalantly bouncing around the garden. She spies the disgustingly joyous and twirling fairy wrens on the fence, letting the spring air puff up their little chest feathers.

She'd placed bets on herself being a great mother. She'd placed bets on this whole maternal thing being way easier. She was obviously in the process of losing all her money.

She listens to the little metal trucks crash into each other on the floor. No more tears come out of her. They seem to have hardened somewhere in her insides, like mush on a highchair. Her eyes are unmoving as they stare around at the kitchen utensils that are spread evenly on the floor throughout her house. If she was a real racehorse and she actually won this high-pressure race, society would award her all the glory, ribbons and prize money. But she's what people call *just a stay-at-home mum.* And these qualitative things are so tricky to measure, there are so many variables ... She starts imagining that every time someone says to her, *Oh, I think it's time you return back to work now* or *You've had your time off,* she imagines rolling over like a retired racehorse, closing her eyes, and listening for the euthanising trigger to click and ripple around the hay-filled stall. And the sound of that click joins all the other collateral and tedious noise of the day.

The Places She Goes Back To

They have fudge in their mouths and mud caked on their boots and they all stand military-like outside the school hall. Today is the leadership preparation day for the Year Fivers. Some of their bodies have been moved around by puberty and their perspiration is now tainted with an unpleasant odour. Some bodies haven't been moved at all and their innocent eyes stare ahead, oblivious. Regardless, it's a vulnerable time for such fledglings. And for just a few brief moments, the sweet glug of fudge in their mouths makes them forget about all this stuff going on inside. Some things are just simple and sweet, like the chocolate fudge that Robbie's mum makes.

The teacher blows her red whistle and Georgia watches a little dribble of slobber flick out the hole of it. She's lovely, this teacher, and Georgia hangs off her every word like a tick on new skin. The teacher announces the next activity: *trust building*, and she needs a volunteer. Georgia's back now bends, trying to stick her arm up straighter than anyone else's. This is her moment to dazzle. She doesn't know what she's volunteering for, but she doesn't care. Adrenaline pulses through her. She really wants to be a leader, like, really badly wants to be a leader. Her tongue quickly tries to rub the brown sticky fudge from her teeth; nothing can get in her way. She pulses her upstretched hand just to draw attention from the others. But another girl is chosen. Georgia slumps.

According to the man with the clipboard, the volunteer has to stand up on a high wooden table and fall backwards and the class has to catch her. Sounds simple enough. Georgia stands with the other girls ready to catch, still nursing her bruised ego. Every now and then she feels another crumb that's stuck on her gums or in between her teeth and the sweetness of the fudge starts to feel a bit sickly in her tummy.

The kids are to stand in a line, two rows, kind of like crocodile teeth. Clanking. Staggered. The volunteer has to stand on the table, back towards the class, shut her eyes and fall backwards. She just needs to trust her peers. Sounds fairly straightforward. But Georgia feels the mechanical mouth of nerves lock its teeth around each girl's waist. She feels it knock along the line like a Mexican wave. Going up the line. Going down the line. The man with the clipboard says to the girls, 'Girls, you obviously aren't as strong as the boys, and therefore you are to be positioned around the bottom half, the legs and feet ...'

Steps ahead of him, the girls have to move very little. They're familiar with everyone's expectations. They're familiar with all of their many, many weaknesses. And they hear the term *girl germs* too many times a day to be ignorant of them. Georgia studies the girls on either side of her and wonders whether boys really are stronger. From where she is standing, most of the girls are actually much bigger than the boys.

'Boys, you are to be positioned further up to catch the backside, back and head.'

Some of the popular boys shudder at the word *backside*. They eyeball each other as if they've been asked to lick a toilet. Most of them know their own potential to inflict harm, and it's as easy as breathing. They sharpen their words like beaks. Every day the teachers reward them for doing one itty bitty task half right. The naughty ones are the scariest and they get the most merit awards. *Keep your enemies closer;* Georgia has seen that tactic at play from early on. She doesn't think it works but she still wants to believe it might.

The exaggerated man pulls himself up onto the table and pats the girl on the arm.

'I promise you, this is perfectly safe. Everyone'll catch you, obviously ... You just need to trust, darl.'

Darl. None of it feels right. Georgia shuffles her boots over the hard-wooden floorboards of the hall. The sickly-sweet fudge is acidic in her throat, threatening to come up. She looks at the weight distribution of the crocodile teeth and worries about the boys' end. The popular boys' end. She wouldn't even trust them to catch her lunch box, let alone a whole human girl.

'Ready ...' he yells.

Georgia hears sniggers to her right.

'Steady ...'

She looks up the line and can see Robbie mouthing to the others: *Pull your hands back ...*

His mouth is like a hellish cavern, drool frothing on his lips, and Georgia can see what she imagines to be Satan waiting there in the dark at the back of his tongue. Georgia shuts her eyes, bracing for impact and, as expected, the crash ripples through her. The girl's head slams onto the hardwood floor. The smashing sound reverberates around the old hall and before Georgia's even opened her eyes she can feel the girl's shaking pant leg now slipping out of her hands.

On opening her eyes, she notices first that many of the boys have stepped very far back, as if a can of repellent has been sprayed between them. They look more shocked than anyone. Their eyes scan for the guilty person to point at, and some of them really believe it was just one person who committed the crime. Secondly, she notices that the girls and a few of the quieter boys are still trying to hold the fallen girl's legs, almost desperately. They're grabbing at the legs even though she's crumpled and inverted, not to help her but perhaps to emphasise the fact that they did the right thing.

Thirdly, Georgia looks at the girl on the floor and she is crying and red and her head is cupped in her hands. The teacher and organiser flock to the girl and silently pray between them that no serious damage has been incurred. Surely this wouldn't be an outcome they should have predicted? The woman's face is white. The adults scan the girl ... she will live. This could have been worse. It's just a knock on the head. The man rubs the girl's head like a bit of grass. That's all. Knock on the head. That's all.

Lastly, Georgia stares into the faces of those around her. Particularly the girls. Not one of them had said anything even though they had all felt the crash before it happened. And none of the girls still holding the legs look shocked at all. Not the least bit surprised. In fact, it's almost impatience that flits across those pubescent cheeks. The girls hold the legs until the teacher tells them to let go. They are obedient more than they are rational. Georgia turns to her best friend and with her fingernails scratches off the dried fudge on her cheek. Hard. Rough. Her friend says, 'Ouch, stop it, Georgia!' but Georgia doesn't stop and she continues to scratch at the skin until every little trace of the chocolate is gone.

Butcherbirds kill their prey and then store the bodies in the forks of trees to save for later. The popular boys are silent while they are yelled at but some of them smirk. Robbie mumbles something under his breath and a few laugh. Their dominance has again been proven. The few quiet boys that did the right thing are grimacing. Pacing. They will have to pay for this later, oh yes, they know the consequences of not following.

'Pussies.' Robbie shoots it at them like he's spitting a golly.

The teachers search for a first aid kit even though there's nothing in there that can really fix this.

And though the girls follow the orders through the next few years, the taste of distrust grows ever sweeter, ever sicklier. Some golden birds with softer beaks do end up proving themselves over time, but not one can completely rid the girls' mouths of all those sickly crumbs. Jammed in between their molars. Stained on their skin. Stuck in all those places Georgia goes back to when she's trying to fall asleep, when sometimes she can't even trust the bed to hold her.

Monopoly

She yanks the suitcase shut and the insides spill. It won't do up. She sits on it. She gets up, cursing at the zippers. All the things she's ever felt boil inside her, bubbling out through her tears and her sweat and her hair from its ponytail. She has had control for so long, her body doesn't know how to function in such a mess.

It's a hurt that is fiercely acute, but she still can't tell you exactly where it is. *Everywhere*, she thinks. *It hurts everywhere. Separation must kill you. Nobody could come out of this alive.*

The bedroom feels vandalised. Cushions have curled. The carpet is in itself an insult, a fat lie. Its expensive wool has brought with it no added softness. Absolutely false advertising. And the fights these plaster walls have witnessed in the past few weeks ... She cringes, remembering those barbed words she released like bullets into the night. Those words could kill a man. She meant every single one of them. And at the same time, she didn't mean any of them.

She can see now the second mortgage was another lofty mount they pursued like it was expected. Like it would never end; just keep buying, keep buying, and the thinness of their living didn't give them any glue to mend their frays. And the tatters wore down too much, too much to hold the two ships together. They had moved in different directions and hadn't even realised. The rope broke and it didn't even matter anymore who broke it. But now there were two little tenders floating nearby, untethered. They were her main worry.

Her two children are playing in the other room, fighting over Monopoly again. Someone's greedy again. But isn't that the point of the game? Don't you have to be, to be the winner? The youngest is yelling.

'Why can't we just buy what we need and keep playing longer? Don't you want to play for longer?'

'No, idiot, I want to win,' the other yells.

The mother already knows she will get the blame for this. At least for a while. She knows you can't put adult weights on the shoulders of children. She would never want even a grain of this pain to dust their cheeks. But what will she say when they ask where they are going? What will she say when they ask to go back home? She runs her overloaded bag out to the old Subaru and throws it in the boot. She'd done the majority of the kids' clothes earlier when they'd been out in the backyard. She'll leave the rest. All replaceable. What aren't are the bits of herself she's leaving suspended in all the pockets of the house, unsaid.

'Kids, finish up that game now.'

She gingerly dances around their doorway. She puts fake warmth into her voice like a Black & Gold bandaid over a deep laceration.

'Nah, mum. Haven't quite beaten her yet. Another 10 minutes should do it ...'

'Get real, you're not even playing fairly, you're just being a greedy pig.'

The youngest one knocks over the silver dog in disgust and the boy retaliates by throwing away her iron. They start pushing each other and the plastic money goes everywhere. The youngest starts crying. Their mother cracks.

'ENOUGH! I've had enough!'

Her voice tears. Tissue paper in her throat. She stands at the door, trying to suck in air and she doesn't even notice the swallow-size tears that slip down her face and splodge on her shirt. There's something in her face that has never been there before.

The kids are frozen. Silence screams through the house. It's almost deafening. Only the dust particles move between them. And all the unanswered questions. She can see she's scared them now.

They've not been to *here* before with their mum. *Here. This.*

'Kids, we're leaving—'

Her voice teeters over the edge of a saucepan, all choky and wet and bubbly. She can't let it spill over. She's hot and so is her breath. Her insides boil. 'We might not come back.' She says it so quick it sounds like a throat clear. The air ate it, so perhaps it can't be so. She turns her back so she is not studied. 'Grab one toy for the road.'

They do what she says. Exactly what she says. And in that moment, rainbows change forever for those kids. The simple seven colours of an arch, the ones they've drawn a thousand times, become an actual spectrum of light, a true optical illusion they'll never understand again. It's not tangible. No longer drawable. There is no gold at the end. And they could never reach the depths that now exist in their mum. In *adults.* They could chase their mum, they could ask her, they could hug her, but they would never know. They both look down at their feet, at the plastic money, the green and red hotels, at anything other than their mum and all the parts of her tears they don't yet understand.

They both sit in the back seat of the car, looking down at their one toy. The older one, the boy, chose a weird jelly ball that splats against glass. He's not even sure why he chose that one, but it was the closest to the door and he wasn't thinking properly. The girl chose her favourite doll, Sally. Sally is getting on in years but still has reasonable hair that hasn't been hacked down to a crew cut like the others.

Their mother scans the house quickly. If she looks too long maybe she'll disintegrate. Maybe she'll turn to soot, float and then blacken this autumn wind. *Get out,* she tells herself. She grabs the doorknob and stands for a few seconds in the door, looking at the yellow of the kitchen's floating floor, feeling this energy one last time, smelling the smells which are distinctly her house. And the front door clicks shut behind her like a full stop.

She looks at her old car and the two quiet kids inside. They both look over at her, almost in a daze.

The second she steps off the front step she enters a liminal zone, an unknown space. Her status: homeless. Alone, with nothing but razors inside her. Her shoes fumble on his old work boots that sit right where they shouldn't. She catches herself. She stares at them for a moment and feels the intensity of the hatred inside of her. How easy it must be to walk in those shoes and leave them wherever you please … She kicks one of them. Both kids stare at her through the car window. She catches herself again, looks at the kids and traipses back to the car.

The drive is the longest drive in her memory, and yet somehow not long enough. Every radio person tries to make her drink the poison of songs. Every melody is sharp. Sometimes she drinks it and she hates feeling it go down. The kids go in and out of sleep. She's still bubbling, the whole way. Waiting to explode. But she never does. She just quietly pulls up outside her Nana Hazel's house. She doesn't move. The town of Pambula is exactly the same as she remembers, all those lifetimes ago. The skyline's still cream and brown and crumbling. The pavement still craggy and pockmarked. The roundabout still popping with pansies.

'Nannyyyy!' the kids squeal.

They undo their seatbelts and open the doors. She watches them run full pelt through the front gate and start battering the front door. Eventually she sees the door pull back and an old figure emerge. Eyes sunken. Mauve skirt and matching floral blouse. Metal walking stick to the side. Cuddles. Glances towards the car. She wonders what they're telling their great nana. The possibilities scare her.

Nana Hazel holds her right hand up above her brows like a visor, trying to get a good look at her granddaughter. There's a moment where the two women, generations apart, gaze at each other. There are no words, as one can't hear and one is inside a car, but there is clear communication between the two. Sometimes one look can cover lifetimes.

The kids are loud as they squabble over the cat doorstop. *Meow, meow, meow.* They run back and forth in front of the orange and white crockery creature. *Meow. Meow.* Nana Hazel whispers something to them. Something about biscuits in the kitchen. And then looks over and waits for the woman in the car to come. The kids scamper off in a hurry. The woman in the car doesn't think her body will take her in there. *Will it buckle now under her weight? Will she die here in the car seat?* As she struggles out of the car on the steep incline of the street, there's a high-pitched sound that grows louder. Piercing. She looks up for the singer and all she sees are bats, bulb-like, strung along the branches of trees. Thousands of them. Black dots along the stems. Some break open and their sticky wings and claws grab at the air, squealing.

She is used to birds here. Flocks of cockatoos and wattle birds, and little bobbing wrens. Not the clingy, screechy clamour of bats. They sing the petrified song of her own heart. And as she walks in the front veranda, it's like the town envelops her in all her many pieces and holds her tightly. The women squeeze each other and the sobs and whispers wash up the hall. A dusty mouse runs in through the open door.

Oblivious (or are they?) to the grief dripping in the air around them, the kids find the old board games down in the back sunroom and are already fighting about what figurine they get.

'You got the dog last time!'

The smell of the old house is comforting. Hasn't changed at all over the years. There is little light in the rooms, and the curtains are almost shut. The lamps are all on, with women's magazines and crosswords on coffee tables under them, half done, half read. A myriad of cheap reading glasses rest on their pages.

Nana Hazel shuffles across the lino and clicks on the gas. The kettle starts to purr straight away and the broken woman sinks into a chair. She listens to that old steel pot boil like a melody she used to love. She watches it puff and huff and whoosh, all energetic and urgent. She notices a tiny part of herself that she'd forgotten long ago creep up to her heart wall and knock on it.

Knock. Knock. Knock.

She feels the eagerness of its clenched fist. She feels it listen to the *lubb-dubb, lubb-dubb, lubb-dubb* of that busy organ, and she wonders whether anyone inside will ever answer that knock again.

Or will it go on knocking forever?

She shakes her head. *Nup. This heart is dead. It's door-knob dead in its dock.*

The steaming Earl Grey seems darker than usual and as if scared, she looks over and watches her Nan snap a Scotch Finger in half. Perhaps it is terror that flares in her eyes now, that everything has changed and she cannot go back, that she's lost her home. Inhale. She labours through each singular breath and her eyes rove. She's searching for something. The tea towels are still all crocheted, hanging over the handle of the stove. The tablecloth still has Alan Border and his cricket bat on it. The cookie jar is still a large, plastic green frog. Her eyes trace the borders of the kitchen, the window, the old lace curtain that hasn't moved in 40 years. She runs her hand over Alan Border's crocheted face and his lumpy moustache and she knows for a fact that nobody else in the world has a tablecloth quite like this one. And then she sees it. That little hand-painted milk jug with the blue bird on it. The woman stares at the bird. It stares at her. And it's as if she is a time traveller wandering through a different era. Perhaps an era when she knew herself and her worth and she desperately wanted the adults to see her. To really see her. Now, her adultness scares her. Her silence scares her and the blue bird scares her. *Imagine still sitting here, staring around this table after all these years. Still bright blue. Still unbroken.*

'Those bats are new, love. Or maybe they've come back after a long time. I can't remember, but they sure are noisy ... and hungry ... and thirsty ...' Nana Hazel smiles as she peers out the window. The tree next door is laden. A black mess through the foliage. Every now and then the bats bicker and squeal. Light brown flecks shine when they rise. Feeble wing bones stretch. 'The last few years they've been staying longer and longer. Guess it's a good place to come back to.' Her soft fingers fumble for some sugar cubes and she plops them into her cup. Adds some milk from the blue bird jug. Stirs with her other hand, using a collector's edition Legacy teaspoon. Every utensil and additive are characters in the narrative. She smiles and shuts her eyes as the steam from her tea fogs up her glasses.

The kids are electric in the sunroom, shouting and zapping in currents ... buying, buying, paying, passing Go, collecting $200, in that race to win again.

The screaming from outside becomes part of the woman and she settles into her soft seat. *Why were we racing?* she wonders. *Who were we racing against?*

She picks up the teaspoon and fingers the red flame of the Legacy emblem at the top of it. She thinks of her parents and her grandparents and all the love that came before her. She sips. It's strong. Almost too strong. But it feels good going down.

'Don't buy Park Lane! You know those ones are always mine!'

'But you don't play fair! Why are the cheap, crappy ones always left for me? I'll buy what I want, thank you very much!'

Nana Hazel smiles towards the backroom, sucking at her soggy biscuit. She chuckles at the yelling and then turns back to her granddaughter, her bent fingers stroking her cup.

'We all learn in time, don't we?'

The newly single woman looks down and realises the more tea she drinks, the lighter the liquid becomes and the surer she is that she's done the right thing. *There's something beautiful about old age, about playing the long game*, she thinks, as she leans over to refill her cup.

Empire (Part Two)

Hold my hand, please   the Fires Near Me app will show new fires   you will see them
like melanoma   your fingers will feel them burn through the screen of your phone   Hold my hand
please   I will take you through a town I once knew   its skyline like a theatre   I watched
the most beautiful shows there   all the different ways   star jasmine twirled in the eaves
            weary suns sunk onto gable windows   and glittered across the glass …

    Paint-chipped walls that told you their stories over and over again in sepia   in polaroid
in finger lime and bottlebrush   and dragonflies   with teapots and fluffy cosies
                and toilets with pull chains.

    The sky above that Yuin land glowed tangy most nights, Little Pony pink, balmy salsa-like fruit bats danced
in the hues   those reeds purred in the wind   as the wetlands dried   and cracked.

My little town, with its soft warm wood and thumb-printed bricks   has nothing to save it now
from the falling ash and embers   When Hell roared through Heaven, I almost wanted it to just come
    come through and be done with it.   That's how long I had been anxious for.   I never want to hear
that ABC radio say   *it's too late to leave*   again for the rest of my life.   I left
because that sentence was too much for me and I ran from that sentence as much as I ran from the fire.
          Claustrophobe, you see.   I packed my surfboard and wanted to paddle to New Zealand …
or another galaxy. But my baby could not paddle. Could not swim.   Could not even breathe at night.

What world was I giving to him?

Hey, Sweet Boy, here's Hell wrapped in a red ribbon. You don't need to unwrap it. It's already here.

There's a hole in my bucket, dear Ibis, dear Ibis
there's a hole in my bucket, dear Ibis, a hole.

Then mend it, dear human, dear human, dear human,
Then mend it, dear human, dear human, mend it.

My surfboard slid off my car when I'd forgotten to tie it on   someone later found it and dropped it
at my front door   undamaged   My neighbour always dropped bags of vegetables ripped fresh
from her garden on my front gate   sometimes choccies for later.   That street where all my lines
marked the concrete   that street where all the things I ever felt were born   where all the words
I'm yet to say were planted like bitty seeds from a book.   Well   this is the   beanstalk

and it's surrounded by flames

          those   f l   a   m   e s   are licking the words right off my to n gue.   . … …

You see, it all hits *us* first. Us, fringe dwellers.

Mrs Mac said to me when I was four   'Stretch, Georgia, stretch 'til the day you die,'   and she pushed
her walking stick into my chest   'Hold that for me,'   she said. My mum said,   'Mrs Mac!
     you're over 100! For goodness sake!'   But I watched her stretch her two arms
right up into the heavens of that shop   (there were heavens there on that ceiling, I remember
     full of stories

buttons   tape measures   & ticking clock hands
and pantyhose-I-knew-I-wanted-to-try-on-when-I-grew-up)   up they went
her hands all bent jigsaw pieces   then floated down   down to the wooden ground   lightly they kissed
her slippers   her winky face looked up at me   Australia's oldest tax payer
           then she slipped those crinkled hands under her feet   as if the earth had no end to it
      there was no ground beneath us   'See the backs of my legs, Georgia.   See, they are not bent.
                    Don't let your body stick.   We are meant to be stretched.'

      I placed the stick down and tried   I shook as I bent over   my fingers twinkled   for my shoes
      there was much sky between my feet and my fingertips   that sky   I learnt   in time
how to hold it   I felt every star   as I breathed in the air that gradually turned too thick   to breathe
                … the mind should never recoil   should never rest at a length
           onwards ever outwards   upwards   should already have gone
inwards

                                        this is your montage

The bluetongue that lives under my bin   what happened to him?   everything I touched ignited

that touch of mine was dangerous   and I didn't realise   all those things I did   as I relaxed
into convenience,   efficiency   progress   is it time   for our promotion?
Everything   I touched   ignited

POOF!

and I didn't realise how hot those fires would burn
my one-metre-long fire blanket   (the 1960s one from my nan)   was a chip packet that shrivelled
in a microwave   I ran
I ran I   r a n   up t h at str e e t   an d   do w nnnn   and i couldn't breathe
for the pain in my chest
I'd forgotten to stretch   I'd forgotten I needed air   to breathe

How did we forget we needed air?

With what shall I mend it, dear Ibis, dear Ibis?
With what shall I mend it, dear Ibis, with what?

You have no idea what that red sky was like in real life. Remember those king parrots that used to love each other in the branches of that tree in the corner? Her green face always asked me for seed. Not just any seed, you know, the good stuff, the chook's stuff. I imagine those two   black now sooty on the sand.   The ash like black vomit from an evil beast. Probably from Hades itself   I had studied their new feathers closely when they perched   on my shoulders.   I knew their smell.   I knew the sound of their wings puffing underneath my ears   my bird friends that saved me but I let them burn   I   RAN   because it was all too much

There were people sprawled, sleeping on treadmills & yoga mats covered by towels & terror & flighty responses & past traumas that resurfaced on people's sooty faces, magicians twirled & tricked kids to pass time with bubbles, dogs barked from cars, horses pooed on the bitumen old people crumbled into the equipment   people tried so hard to help — the clubs were Noah's Ark & my phone *ding ding dinged* all day … if only there was a downpour … but it couldn't have been dryer. The app looked like it had measles. Nobody had nappies. A stomach bug passed around the evac centre like a secret. We humans — desperate for anything

frightened of everything. Some expected a cruise ship, some a life raft, all just needing company.
The lifesavers truly wondered whether they could save this many lives if they had to ...
                                                                        Are you still holding my hand?

I thought I'd be hot   but I am cold   the wind is so hot it makes the baby hair
    on my face curl   it makes my baby cough all night, all night   dear Ibis   all night
    you haven't   heard   a   sound   so   terrible

the guilt of it has opened up something in me   that can never will never
ever not be an open catastrophic hole   I will continually fall into   I can tell

a mother   is not the prime minister

    and my heart burns cool   by now I think it has gone numb   my skin just porcelain cold   catches
the embers   I've never been a rule breaker   rules make me feel safe.   That's why I write
        because every piece has its own rules   but this   I guess the universe has its own rules
            rules we broke and break   in extraordinary ways

because   money

and now these fires on every side   have no rules   They have left some houses   for no reason
        they have burnt some   for no reason   right to the ground   they have burnt whole species
        whole towns, dear Ibis   whole   people.   I watched them
  in   photos   and on the news   chase all the unicorns into the sea like that red bull

                              each-of-these-towns-is-an-organ-in-the-one-body

and when I saw they'd cancelled the Cobargo Folk Festival on Facebook   I knew things would never
be the same   not even music

        listen now to 'The Last Unicorn' by America   go on   watch the movie as well   you'll see it
        … that was my favourite movie when I was four and five and six and 12 and 15.   I never knew
I'd meet that bull at 34   the redness of that sun like a sad, dangerous disc   that melts into the sea
            we   were   chased   into   the   sea   the   world   watched   us   glow   red   on   their   TVs
while chomping their UberEATS   but were you holding my hand or was I holding yours? Or were we
packing   our   bags   and   throwing   them   into   the   cars,   our   hearts   beating   from   our   puffing   cheeks?

What do we take? What will we need?   But were we hot or cold? I only remember the smoke
that sauntered in my ears   and filled my brain   a fog   no intelligence remained   no words
could stick there   none significant   or sensible

          every night of my life that I couldn't sleep   the inevitability of the coming day   always soothed me
               it was the only thing I could ever be sure of growing up
                    — that day would always follow the night.

     Oh, but Ibis …   daylight didn't follow night   it didn't come for days.

     That movie *Melancholia* really got it. There's something about that sister's husband … as I pace
my veranda watching my own otherworldly swollen moon   so red / my blood   I grasp the power
of art   that moment when he realises   he is wrong   insanely wrong   he commits suicide
          the cognitive dissonance of it all   Overdosed   until   it was dissonant no more
just like Hitler killed himself   denial then and now was is genocide   We had a chance to stop the mass
extinction, they'll say, just before it ends   I'd rather it be art, dear Ibis, dear Ibis. I'd rather it be art
                              Dear Ibis   just art.

People on the TV say these are just buildings   you can replace buildings

                              I hear your words   but you didn't hear   all the stories
that sat in their fibres   you never smelt the paint on that wood   you didn't feel   the floorboards creak
in those sacred spots as you paced   you didn't feel the ghosts hug you when you cried   you didn't know
them like I did   you didn't rest your head against the uneven, softness of that cedar   that cedar
from 1880   and feel the love of the hands that individually sanded and nailed those panels there.
You didn't trace the outline of that building with your own two ageing eyes every hour of every day
of every year of every unfinished sentence that the outline held   I could feel the secrets tinkling off
their gutters on a sunny day from across the street and every day it looked different   and made me feel
different   you don't know how many times I changed the colour of my front door   just to tell a story
        People need stories

    Hold my hand, please I will take you through my home   until the fires get so hot
and the winds push the flames all over you   'til you can do nothing but surrender to them.
    I know I lit them.   All of them.   If   you'll   all   stop   blaming   each   other   you'll   see
    I am taking full blame.   Maybe then you can have a conversation   include everyone
    and make a plan.

I'm so tired of everyone yelling and venting in an angry deadlock. Be angry at me. I'm nothing
        but an artist   so I have nothing   else to lose now. I can take it all.   Now you please go
and despite all this blackness, please take action. Let go of my hand!   Look   at   your   own   hands
        what wonders can they do now ?   Scrape the ash from your nostrils and run! Feel the rain
come   and one day you'll see green. I know you will.   But I want you to remember this blackness
                                Never forget the part you played in this dismal avant-garde theatre show —
        the apocalypse, we all called it   nobody clapped at the end

                                                        everybody just yelled at each other for a long time.

And Blair's Tower just stood   out the end   no trees remained   like a huge Cubist phallus
        not even the end of the world could cut that ego down   I stared at it   for a long time
from Cogra Beach   my kid on the soot-covered playground   and sun on my brow   the birds in front
of me wading through the water   that tower again

        completely by itself.

We are human and ibis no longer   maybe our narratives are too scorched together now
        I can't see where the feathers stop and the skin begins

Then mend it, dear human, dear human …

    Where I'm going I won't let my body stick, I will stretch daily.   And when I become a Planeteer
I will ask for the wind ring. I know it is the wind I want to control now.   I am not fit
to control people's hearts. I am not sure anyone is. And that's the beauty of hearts   everyone is free
to choose   but one lie becomes many   I've seen it   one problem leads to another
because we really did make error upon error   how far back does it go?   Listen to that white noise
and stand on your feet now   cause the stakes are so high, Dear Ibis

        Even though I can't tell you what to do
    I can tell you that water can't put out all fire   burning won't burn all fuel
        some fires come from the darker spaces of a human heart
        those ones the scientists can't seem to negotiate with
        those ones that build the empires
                                they are the ones to watch

Empire (Scene Three of Script)

A human stands in an enormous gravel pit, unsure of where they are or who they are. Unsure whether the air is suitable to breathe. Unsure where everyone and thing has gone. There's a dying ibis lying in the dirt to the side; its charred feathers have melted into the earth. There is an old bucket off to the side of the human with a little but very visible hole in the bottom of it.

Human: There's a hole in my bucket, dear Ibis, dear Ibis.

Dying Ibis: There always will be, dear human, dear human …

(Ibis voice trails off)

The human looks frustrated, confused. It walks to the edge of the gravel pit and stares down into a wasteland. There is nobody and nothing alive. Not even a film crew or camera person to film it in this expanse.

Human: I don't get it. What's the point of going through this crap if it isn't filmed, marketed or sold?

The dead ibis does not answer. Too dead now or something. The human walks from that side of the gravel pit to the other and stares down into another expanse of wasteland.

Human: (Yelling) Hello? What's the point of anything if there's nobody here to 'like' it? What's the bloody point? Anyone out there?

Two days pass and the wind howls dust into every corner of the gravel pit. Little tornadoes form around the human. On the third day the wind ceases and not a breath remains. Everything is still and empty.

The human walks over to the dead body of the bird. The human peels the bird off the ground and holds its decomposing body against its face, trying to smell something, anything that has had life in it. Some remaining feathers detach themselves from the rotting body and float to the ground. The eyes are hollow caverns without even a maggot alive to eat at it. In the hands of the human, the bird body seems to float off like dry powder into the air.

Human: Dear Ibis, dear, dear Ibis, this isn't what I wanted … this isn't what I wanted …

Then the human dangles its legs over the highest edge of the gravel pit, hugging the ibis desperately like a ragged doll. From this height, the human can see the whole world. Not a thing alive remains. Just infinite nothingness. The human cries. Not from what has happened, not from what it can see, not from there being holes in a bucket, but from it being completely alone.

Antagonist

There it is. A bird with a cotton ball chest, frozen in place. The reeds whisper and blow to the side and the bird doesn't move. Still and solid as the metal sculpture above it. The wetlands are to the right, and the sun is blazoned as it bounces off the water. The light of the morning touches everything in warm yellow; even the trees look gilded. Is this even real? The bird, I mean. Nothing can stand that still, can it? I guess if it is the protagonist of this story then it's about to do something really good.

As I move closer, I start to make out its curved lines ... how its beak scoops downwards like a melting spoon. Its body is pin-cushion perfect. The head and beak, swan-black, rest atop its cirrus body. There's something very familiar about its stooped head. I'm so close to it now I can see it's a girl bird, and some of the white feathers on the top of her back jump up in the breeze. She's very pretty, that I'm sure of.

Yep, it's a white Australian ibis, that's clear now. To prove she is not a statue, she cocks her head to one side and studies me like a road sign. Her forked feet do not move on the glary concrete. She casts no shadow, which makes me think she might just be the antagonist of this narrative.

It is alarming when her beak separates and she starts to speak.

'And what happened to *you*?'

I look down at myself embarrassed. *To me? What does she mean?*

Her narrow eyes travel up and down my body and there's something alluring about her assertiveness.

'I said,' and with this she squints her eyes and pushes her head forwards towards me, '*What* happened to *you*?'

I watch her long beak separate like two wires in love – and I think I am actually in love.

I look down at my feet and realise they are forked like hers. What the – why are my feet forked? There's a chewing gum wrapper stuck to one of my toes. What happened to my normal feet? I follow the forks up, up, these spindly and scabby black legs to my white plume. Surely not ...?

The white ibis at the wetlands entrance has not lost her focus.

'You there, I asked you a question ...'

My cheeks heat up as I look down at my feathers that are ravaged, torn-at and wispy. What *did* happen to me? I look like an ibis but I'm different ... scabbier, aged, almost trashy. Is this all a dream? Can a dream even work as a short story anymore? Isn't that just lazy writing?

The end of my beak seems savage, like a black butcher's hook. I'm quite slick, but cracking like a blister and the only thing I'm sure of is that the dialogue is coming from the ibis. The white, unruffled one. I'm not sure who the protagonist is. It must be me.

My insides whip and flare with heat and lust and I feel a bit messy; I've never seen a more exquisite creature. I edge closer. If I am the protagonist and she is the antagonist, I'd better brace myself. I feel all shameful and sorry but I don't know what for. Maybe my appearance? My tummy is coiled in a knot. I'd been just picking at my usual garbage bins near Central Station in Sydney this morning when this guy threw me – my ibis self, I mean – into the back of a truck. I was picking near some bags of stuff and then I felt these hands on me and then Bob's your uncle, I was chucked in this dark cabin. I don't think the man knew I was in there. He was in a hurry and wasn't paying attention to what he was doing. Many hours later, the truck pulled up here. The driver ate a sandwich and had a walk around. Somehow I was plucked out of the cabin and thrown on the pavement, staring at this beautiful bird. Maybe it was a writer who did it? I'm not really sure. I thought I was human, but it's clear I am a bird. I've had quite the day, reader ...

'Excuse me, are you quite OK? No offence, but you look ... a bit sick?' Her head shakes in frustration, or maybe it's to show off her perfect plume. 'Hey there, I'm talking to you!'

It's clear now as she lifts her head that she's a bit taller than me. Her surroundings have allowed her to surpass me. Typical. She seems better than me in every way.

As I peer down in front of me at my pointy head and beak like a stroke of petrol I can feel the bitter chunks in my joints. I start to feel the gross centipede of trauma crawling around my insides. I don't even know which landslide it crawled out of, to then find shelter in my cavities. Is it even all mine? All those diseases, disabilities, death and neglect. All that detachment. All that lonely rain that never eased. And then the disability that became my own. It's in this body now, I can feel it. To be honest, I've done well just to show up here.

I scan the perfect wetlands and its easy-peasy weather and I scoff. *If I lived here, I'd be perfect too.* I shake the chewing gum wrapper off my weird foot.

And then I glare back at that boring ibis with no love. I feel my shadow long and dark beside me but it feels more like art.

'Do I need to say it ag—'

'No!' I say, my own black tweezer lips adding to the dialogue.

It's alarming but reassuring to hear my own voice for the first time. I edge nearer, leading with my chest. My eyes narrow. And the admiration I felt earlier for her is now mine, all mine. My scars, like silk, thread into lace and cover my body. She has saved nothing for later. She is all that you see. Though I didn't plan it I think the climax is coming like a season change, but I really don't know what will happen. I plod towards the water, ignoring the other bird. When I get there it is still, and for the first time I can see myself. My curves are delicate, and it's impressive the way my head dips and my beak hooks and my chest rises and my legs support me, unwavering. My white chassis is textured and full of treasures. My black frills and cognition, close to full functioning – I am high achieving. I am strong. I can survive in trash and I can tell my story proudly to people who don't even care. I see myself. Not as sub-par. Not as scabby. Not as damaged. But as a protagonist, a fully rounded, interesting and animated character who is good enough to compel a reader. I can flesh out a book, tell my own story. I'm strong enough to create debate, to challenge the status quo. I refuse to be easy on the eye. I chew the truth like it's no big thing and swallow it like something I was built to transform. And as I dip my forked toes into the water, my muscle memory starts to bring it all back ...

Water like this used to be mine. Up near Sydney. Sometime over the last 50 years or so. And then there's this other part of me that I can feel, my non-bird self, that bulldozed it all. My human self built big human things there. My human self wanted to grow, to evolve, to become successful. I cleared those wetlands, and it felt good. Felt civilised. Powerful. I felt like I was someone. Like I was leaving a legacy. I was doing my job and paying bills and following orders. It was like I had become the ultimate hero in Joseph Campbell's journey. The machines were the supernatural aids and the environment was the threshold and I pushed through and everything transformed.

My bird self did not stay and watch my family flapping and flying away, bewildered. I just focused on my human progress and nothing else. Each marsh I ploughed through felt awesome. The birds … they sorted themselves out, eventually. My ibis self just grew quiet. Many other species just carked it. But not me, not us, we adapted. We proudly became bin chickens. We learnt how to split open the plastic bags and puncture garbage bags easily with our claw feet. I filed my scissor beak down to a fine tweezer-like point to be more accurate. More precise. My newly filed beak allowed me to pincer the smaller, yummy-scrummy things in the skip bins. I can still fish in the swamps and gutters like old times; you couldn't take that from me if you tried. We bred up. Almost became Australia's favourite bird last year. Beaten only by the magpie. It's just a matter of time though. We will prevail.

I look back at what we came from, the great Australian White Ibis. There's something greatly dissatisfying now to perfection. I expect her to be more than that. I'm not interested in her statuesque stance or how unblemished her feathers are. I want more.

A red belly black snake wriggles between us on the hot concrete. We both stare at it as if someone has just placed a line between us. The ibis, she's quizzical now. Almost sympathetic, with one claw raised, head lower. She seems to be thinking of her next row of dialogue, where I'm sure the subtext will be, *you look disgusting, you are less than, you are messy* …

'I know what happened to you,' she concedes, almost sadly, 'you're a bi—'

'Bin Chicken,' I say.

I won't let *her* say it. She won't talk for me anymore.

'I'm a Bin Chicken.' I puff out my chest and I can almost feel her admire my buoyancy as I swagger past. She looks a bit affronted, like she's changing her mind about something.

'Of course, of course.'

Of course. What's that supposed to mean? Like she's the only educated one, fit enough to classify me. I watch her smooth her wing with her beak, and readjust her plumage.

And then as if it is the next expected thing to say, she adds, 'So, do you want to live here with us? It's lovely and there's heaps of room … reckon you could do with a sea change …'

She motions with her beak towards the marshes and now I'm looking clearly I can see a few other ibises there, swimming and slurping.

I was not prepared for her kindness. I step backwards and the snake on the ground tilts its head round to look at me. I ruffle my wispy wings and then I ruffle them again, looking for grounding. I feel guilty for all the mean things I thought about her. And here I was thinking I was the evolved one. I guess I was looking for the enemy, for the tension. And she was the only other one here.

'Hang on,' I say, bothered, 'But I thought *you* were the antagonist in this story?

'Me? Honey, we are all some kind of ibis. Why would you go looking for enemies?'

I shrug, embarrassed. 'I just thought that's how stories worked?'

'Maybe where you're from it is a bit more cut-throat, each bird for themselves maybe. We don't think like that. We're pretty chill here. As long as we remember our place and don't mess with it, the more the merrier. We think about the group. Everything is connected. And we've got everything we need here. Come on in.' She turns her body slightly away from me as though looking for something. Then her head swivels back to me, 'What's wrong? You look flushed or something …'

It is here that the narrative becomes more confusing because her squeaky bird voice interlaces with some sort of human voice from my past. The air streaks with paint as if it's suddenly 2D. The snake stops looking at me and wriggles off frantically, and the other ibis, well, she vanishes. A wisp of cirrus white is left floating in front of me as I wake.

The conclusion is an odd one because as I write neither of the protagonists remain. Just me. A strange interloper. A white, privileged human in my warm linen sheets. I pull myself up in the bed and turn to face the mirror. I have a good look. I do not look away. I look at myself as if in third person. I can see all the redness, the bed hair. I stare at my closed mouth. Such a rarity for it to be closed.

I try to look through myself, all the way to the other side. It's hard, at first, to see what's there, on the other side of me. I don't know how long I stare for but it feels like days, weeks even, months. And then, after all the golden light, all the feathers, all the banter, all the dreams, I finally reach the psychological shift of the story. I wasn't the protagonist. I had been the antagonist here all along.

The Plovers Get Louder!

Ed scrawls across the paper with a crayon, *WIGWAM FOR A GOOSE'S BRIDLE, MUM, — ED.* He laughs at his own handiwork and then sings out to his younger brother.

'Hurry up Billy!' and much quieter this time, he adds, 'Don't let mum see ya get the gun!'

Billy's 10-year-old arms stretch upwards, his fingers fumble for the pea-rifle. Tendrils of snot drip from his nostrils right down to his lips and his bear-brown hair juts into his eyes at uneven intervals. He strains with all the gusto of a fighter on the frontline.

The rifle hangs on an old nail on the back of his mum's bedroom door, just out of the boys' reach. Or so their mum thinks. Billy's tongue is out now, and the snot pools onto it. His calves are tight to the point of bursting, and his whole body is tense like a hound's. They need the gun. Those ruddy rabbits need to be taught a lesson. With a loud grunt, he edges the rifle off the nail and catches it coolly before it clatters to the ground.

'Goddddiiiit!' he sings, gullumping up the hallway and disappearing down the front steps.

Veronica pulls up her calico dress and plops herself onto the lavatory. The lace on her bottom hem drags in the dirt ... She tries to remember a time when she was able to administer to such things as a lace hem. The boys and the farm take up all the space in her brain. *It's a blasted curse becoming a mother in this world, this world where you have no say in nothin'. After all the sickness, danger and soreness of growing a wee tot, women'd never see any harm come to those babes. It's a love that hurts right down to the stringy fibres of our cores,* she thinks. She'd lock them in a cage if it would mean they'd be safe. But she couldn't handle them unhappy… *to see their wings clipped like the chooks just wouldn't be right …*

She pulls up her bloomers and hurries out, knowing full well she needs to find time to empty that blinking can but she knows she can't leave the boys unattended too long. Their naughtiness has been increasing by the day and with Tom off fighting (saving his country on the Western Front; a place called Pozières was what he put in his letter), Lord knows what those two will be like when he returns. If he returns.

Everything feels like it's slipping away. All her pretty things squandered. She knows she looks like the Wreck of Hesperus but she pushes that aside. Any settledness she'd ever felt now is dashed. Her heart races like a brumby on a ridge. It's bedlam. And the more those boys race, the faster her brumby races, its hooves always skirting a cliff edge.

Like two little blowflies, they flap through the grass. Fence to fence, boundary to boundary. Two buzzing dots on a mission. They roll under the barbed wire in swift movements, no trouble at all. Billy is careful, always keeping the long gun close and upright like a tin soldier.

While their dad's at war, blowing things up in France, they don't need potholes forming in the paddocks. Don't need the sheep's food being poached by bunnies. *To hell with 'em,* Ed thinks. And they taste bloomin' good in a stew. Win win. Nope, their mum wouldn't like it, no doubt about it, but imagine her face when him and Bill bring them home, swinging from their lapels! Even their mum couldn't deny them a big mighty stew. Ed tells Billy about the funny note he left for their mum using the phrase their parents so often used. Ed thought he had used it correctly. *None of your business, mum* ... they both chuckled. But the humour of Ed's smart aleck note fades as Ed trudges on and he starts to worry ... should he be the one holding the gun? Has their mum noticed their absence yet? He wonders how much trouble they'll be in when they get home ...

Veronica hurls herself out of the outhouse, quicker than Fanny Durack at the Olympics. She flies through the backyard, and races up the side of the house. There's silence. A deadly sound. She knows something's not right when there's silence. It's the worst sound in the world. She cries their names but she knows they're not there. Before she enters through the front door she casts glances right and left, peers through the trees and across the paddocks, looking for signs of them. Nothing. Nothing except a messy note on the door from Ed. *WIGWAM FOR A GOOSE'S BRIDLE, MUM ...* damn that little ... She throws it to the floor. The very real beast has now secured its claws around her lungs and is squeezing them, squeezing them until she struggles to find any air at all.

She dashes up the hallway towards her room, flings open her door and she already knows the gun is gone. She gasps at the nail and screams pointlessly into the nasty void that has become her house. The sound that comes out of her does not feel like her own but someone else's. It is too primal, too hysterical, too animal-like to be hers.

All her boys are out of her reach and her limbs have turned to jelly. She can't breathe. Everything is a shadow. Everything is a trick.

'BIIILLLLYYYYYYY! E-E-E-EDDDDDDIIIEEEEE!'

Her shrieks bounce off the wooden walls and go no further. She has no neighbours out here. She tries to focus. *Think, Veronica, think.* Trembling, she rings the telephone exchange and Lucy puts her through to Doctor Charles at the hospital. He will come. He will come and fix whatever damage they manage to do by then. She listens for the inevitable gunshots but all she can hear are plovers. She's got nothing but bullets in her belly. Big deadening bullets, rambling around like prophecies. Like dice in a rattle. And she's not feeling the least bit lucky.

Yowaka River casually saunters by with its yellow glow and frisky mullet. The boys slide on rocks and trip on driftwood. They jeer at scuttling crabs and they try to push each other over. Ed has forgotten to worry and Billy has relaxed his clench of the gun. It flips and flops around by Billy's side, the leather strap dangling over one shoulder. Now that their dad is away, they are the men of these paddocks. They have the world to roam. The world to protect. The world to shoot at.

The boys tear up the hill through the long spinifex grass. The lake is off to their left, flashing in the sunlight, almost too bright to see. They reach grass and their speed increases. And as they leave the road and hurtle down the other side of the hill towards the lake, the sound of a plover's *kekekekek* starts up around them. Ed can see one of the birds shooting at them through the sky, eye level, a grey and white missile ... like morse code. Like a weapon.

'We've gotta gun, ya nitwit!' Ed bellows at it.

The swooping plover misses Billy by centimetres and the boys duck and keep running.

'I hate them bloody birds!' Billy yells as he scoots through the grass.

Sheep eye them off on their left and right and continue chewing. *Such stupid animals*, Ed and Billy think, as they dart past. All woolly and bleaty. All feeble and following. *Baaaa, baaaaa*, they yell back at them, laughing. Their own dominance is intoxicating as they leap onto big boulders and pounce off, as if attacking the air.

Up ahead is Hart's Creek, the edge of their property. A long time ago Billy declared it was called Fart's Creek and that is what it will forever be now to them. For a moment they pause and try to squeeze out a fart. Billy succeeds but Ed just pretends. They squeal with laughter as Billy wonders whether anything followed through into his underwear.

They reach the wooden gate before the water and Ed leaps first, his hands grab the top wooden beam and his legs follow half a second later. Smack into the bottom beam. He clambers like an ant, little but fierce, up and over. Once he gets to the top of the gate he jumps off and his chunky body plops like a sack of coliban potatoes into a patch of grass. Then he turns to watch his brother.

Before Ed can warn him, Billy has forgotten the gun's potential and has turned all his attention to his speedy gate dismount. He must land further ahead than Ed, he must land smoother, he must do it all better than his older brother. His competitive edge never wanes. He leaps, not a worry in sight, the gun like a rucksack knocking beside him. Ed scurries to the side to miss him. The grass is like Gran's cushions beneath him. And Billy's dismount is velvety smooth. The distance cleared seems indeed more than his brother's. But his landing is loud. Louder than it should be.

Deafening like a whip crack.

As Billy lands, the gun blows. Both boys shudder. Their eyes meet, mouths ajar. The thing has gone off and the bullet's destination is for a half-second unknown …

Ed jumps up to standing. Billy follows and falls, grabbing his middle. The blood that starts to pour into Billy's hands is no joke. The gun has got him good. Got him fair in the innards. No doubt about it.

Ed shudders at the bang still ringing in his ears and the smoke that hangs like a mad fever between them. No words are uttered. And then they stare around looking, waiting, hoping for an adult to show themselves. Billy holds his gut casually as if the bullet is just in there temporarily, like it's just a little gut ache that will pass. His face is different, though. Sort of like the lamb's face before his dad kills it for Sunday roast. A few minutes pass before they accept they are alone out here. No-one's coming.

Ed tears off his shirt and jams it over Billy's middle, more to stop the sight of the blood than anything. He can't concentrate with all that red. *Oh, the trouble we'll be in,* he thinks.

Billy doesn't speak but already Ed can hear his breath like a tied-up dog, wincing and wheezing to be let off.

'Lie down, Bill. That's it. That's it. She'll be right, Bill. I'm here. Ssshh. Ssshh.'

Ed is not sure. There are streams of tears gushing off his own chin and onto Billy's face and he's just not sure what this all is. Will Billy die out here like a stupid rabbit? Will he run out of breaths here in the long grass? Should he leave him to go and get help? Flag someone down up the road? He just doesn't know what to do. He decides he should go and get help but his body stays holding Billy. His body does not move.

Billy watches Ed like a wedgetail. Wary, savage, raw. Billy's breath rattles louder and louder and his body moves like a car motor, bubbling and boiling in Ed's bonnet arms.

Doctor Charles picks up Veronica along the highway in his horse and dray. He's talking but she's not hearing a word. He's telling her the boys'll be fine but she's not listening. They're travelling much slower than she'd like. Every metre feels like a year.

She loses sight of the river and the lake comes into view. Rolling green hills. Bracken. Spinifex. A teeny creek. 'Stop!' She squeals and ejects herself out of the dray and sets off running. She doesn't care that the cart is still moving.

Charles pulls the horse to a halt and watches Veronica run wonkily through the rough terrain. He's bemused and before too long he reluctantly follows her, his medical kit in tow. He's following her strict instructions, but he knows he won't need the kit. *Mothers worry so much*, he thinks. *I'm a placebo for her and that's OK*, he thinks. *This is what this whole 'rural placement' is about*, as he follows her lead.

Veronica can sense her boys near, somewhere near Hart's Creek. She has overheard them chortling about killing rabbits down there. Late, late at night when they think she's fast asleep, some motherly subconscious ear can hear them and their plans. Shooting rabbits, like dad, down near that creek they call Fart's Creek. She often told herself it was all just normal motherly fears, but somewhere deep inside she always knew she had a superhuman, invisible ear that heard all things. And even though she knows she'd told them umpteen times not to ever take the gun and not to ever go out without telling her, she knows where they have gone. She screams out their names. She does not breathe ... breathing is for mothers with their kids safely in their arms ... breathing is for people not in war. What is it with men and guns, with humans and power?

She hears them. She feels them. Ed's screams take her back to when he was very young, to when he was hungry and they'd run out of food. She spies them crouched over near the gate, Ed holding Bill like the Pieta.

Veronica flies towards them, her lacey hem catching on branches and blackberry bushes. White threads are pulling in all directions. She leaps over the gate as if the last twenty years were dreams only and her body is lithe like silk. Ed turns and sees her and the relief is clear on his face, as if his tears are now real and not just shock, as if his mum can turn back time or just apply a salve that can fix this.

She circles the boys in her wings and she squeezes them in to her. She holds them, listening for their heart beats, smelling their smells which are only theirs, watching their chests move up and down. She feels herself become whole again. She knew it was Billy. Deep in her heart's furthest pocket, she knew it would only be him. She always knew she hated guns. She knew the potential for all this a long time ago, like a ravenous fault line next to a rickety cot.

The doctor attends, sweatily gripping his medical kit. His face shines white like the porcelain of a chamber pot, his legs tremble beneath him. His first posting ... in this ragged country, with these limited resources and this bulleted belly before him.

The doctor cups his own face in his hands, rubbing the sweat off and checking his own features as if they have run off scared. *Stay calm*, he tells himself, *stay very calm*. He slightly moves Ed and Billy's hands from the wound and peers in through the gristly blood. Charles takes a moment to consider.

He peers into the dark cavern. Deep. Down. And gently touches the walls of the tunnel with his index finger. He tries to ignore the rattling breaths of the boy and the god-awful plover above him. And then he finds the lead, and his finger traces it, learning where it is and how it will be.

'Ed?' the doctor says, as sweat beads on his top lip and glistens in the sun.

The boy stares up at him, still holding his brother for dear life. With the wound open, the blood now seeps through Ed's shirt to his hands. He notices how warm it feels as his bare chest heaves for air in the searing sun.

'Mmm?'

Charles scans the area. He searches. He sweats. His finger still blocks the hole. *These are the critical seconds*, he thinks, *these are the critical seconds.* He turns to Ed, and though absolutely nonsensical, he chooses his course.

'You need to go and kill a sheep. Shoot it in the noggin.' He points to his own forehead. 'You need to drag it back here very carefully. Don't knock it on anything. Keep it completely intact.'

He looks at Ed's startled face.

'It is very important you do this exactly as I've said ... and quickly.'

Ed is confused but he nods, grabs the pea rifle and scampers off like an injured field mouse. Veronica paces and hovers.

Charles with acute precision sets up a makeshift operating space with cloths from his kit. He wipes all of his surgical equipment to remove any collected dust. He dunks some in straight alcohol. He also takes a swig. Just to remind himself he can absolutely do this. He doesn't need knowledge now, he just needs confidence.

The shot of the gun somewhere off to the right ripples through them all. Billy winces as if he's been hit again. His breaths are laboured but still drag raspily in and out of his mouth.

It's a bloody perfect sheep, Charles thinks to himself. Ed has shot it fair and clean in the top of the neck and dragged it still twitching through the scrub. The path of blood twinkles in the blistering sun and the smells of blood coalesce. There is a forceful *kekekekekekek* of plovers off near the creek and the doctor tries to ignore the heinous sound.

'Sorry, I tried for the head but—'

Doctor Charles holds his hand up to shush him. He tries to imagine only silence. His scalpel splits the guts of the sheep and a gush of innards seep out into his hands. He wrestles them like snakes, feeling their warm life teeming. He finds the right one, the right bit. Goo and globs cover his skin and the cloth in a matte red. He cuts off about 10 centimetres of entrails. He squeezes the insides out like sewage from a pipe and wipes the blood off the tube until it's pale.

Turning to Billy now, with giant's tweezers, he plucks the bullet from its tummy cave. They all listen to it clunk into a dish. He has never felt this much blood in his nostrils. It's a smell he won't forget quickly. This whole thing is new. Charles has not read about it in books. He's not heard about it from professors. This is new territory and he can feel it bristling his neck with fear and adrenaline. If he can pull this off, he'll be all over the papers tomorrow morn.

Like a butter knife into freshly baked scones, he casually but quickly cuts into Billy's gut and finds the intestines and the bit that's punctured. He can hear Billy's breath weaken, like a dying swallow, fluttering, falling, pausing. Charles cuts, he cuts, he joins, he sews. Cuts and cuts, and joins, and sews.

He studies the joins and he nods. He breathes. He takes a

moment, hands poised above the scene, to breathe slowly, deeply. He shuts his eyes and opens. The scene looks frightening but he thinks of his Granny Pat when he was a boy teaching him to sew. Her words come back to him, *Watch the needle, Charlie, don't rush*. He tugs the string slightly to check. His grandma would be proud. Everything is where it should be; he closes the skin like an envelope and with the same needle begins his grandma-style darning. He pauses, takes another swig of alcohol and feels the liquid heat him, pat him on the back, and revitalise his bloodied vision. He knots the thread. Tells his heart to settle. He takes an enormous gulp of air and holds onto it as if it can float him up and away. As if by some miracle, this wild gamble will pay off. Maybe his Granny Pat is here with him. He can almost smell her lavender scent. *The moment is almost spiritual*, he thinks, and he'd given up on that rubbish long ago.

Ed, Veronica and Doctor Charles carry Billy back to the dray; Charles holds him under the shoulders, taking the weight of his torso and head, and Veronica and Ed take his legs. They sprawl him out in the cart and then squeeze in next to him, watching his chest for a rise and fall.

'You bloody stay with us, Billy Bell. Don't you leave us. You hear me?' Veronica yells into Bill's face as the plovers fade off into the distance.

A few days later, Billy is still sleeping, unable to move, strapped down to a scratchy, hard hospital bed. Veronica is even more emaciated than before. She kneels by the bed, exhausted. Quivering. Empty and tense, on the frontline of her own war. She weeps and wails and goes in and out of talking about Billy and then talking about her husband. Her ranting increases, swelling into peaks and sinking into troughs, and then drifts off again like spume into the sea. She creaks to a stand and paces the room, dawdling at the window.

'How dare they take our men? How dare they leave us all here ...'

She folds her arms, her mumbles deepening.

'Who invented guns, anyway?' she trails off. Still sniffing and shaking. Her dress still pulled and hanging on the floor, ferns and burs all through it, still speckled with blood sprays. She has not left the room since they got there. She paces, huffing, breaking, squawking like a lapwing.

Ed continues holding Billy's hand and checking his breathing. Billy's eyelashes flutter. His eyes open and stretch, guzzling in the room. Stars start to twinkle again in those eyes, like quartz in a riverbank. *It's all good*, Ed thinks. *Everything's going to be OK ... no doubt about it.*

Billy gingerly pats his stomach and feels layers of padding there. He winces. He looks from his mum to Ed and then leans over as much as his bed and tubes will allow, and whispers ...

'How much trouble we in, brother?'

Ed's eyes widen. He leans in, so close to Billy he can smell the alcohol on his skin. He can smell Billy's unwashed body.

'Bill, let's just say, I think we're both gonna wish we *was* dead.'

'Mmm. Thought so.' Billy winces with pain as he slowly wiggles his bum up to a higher position in the bed. His whispers puff out of his lips like little clouds Ed can hardly catch. 'Every time I shut my eyes I hear them damn plovers, like I'm back there. Do you reckon they were warnin' us or somethin'?'

'Settle down, Bill, think you might've knocked your head as well ... You've got a plover right here in this room who's gonna swoop you good and proper if you let her see you're awake!'

Billy nods and then quietly shuts his eyes and pretends to be back, unconscious.

Veronica is still mumbling at the window. She watches the white fluffy chest of a plover strut back and forth next to the hospital entrance. Those birds had always bothered her when she hung the washing out. She sees herself now in that bird, nagging, fighting to be left alone by predators. Aching for peace. *Love is really the most terrifying thing,* Veronica thinks, her face pressed against the glass. Perhaps clipping wings *is* a necessity in this world. Perhaps we need all these restrictions because the world we've made is so full of bangs and violence. She winces at the volume of the *kekekeks* and she wonders whether they are even loud enough ...

A horse outside paws the ground. A kid wails from the dray, clutching at his arm. Veronica watches the mother herd the wailing kid into the entrance, holding a baby to her breast. She turns from the window and sees the fresh flowers nurses have put by the bed. Three tubes of bottlebrush stand in a jar and soften the sterility of the room. They make her smile, her first in three days. Then she looks over at her boys holding hands on the stark bed sheets. Ed's face looks different, somewhat smug. And Billy's face looks like it's *pretend asleep.*

With force she rushes to the other side of the bed and clenches Billy's other hand. And as if her body is nothing but feathers, she puffs and stretches herself around her boys, in love.

'Wigwam for a goose's bridle, hey?' she whispers, as the boys wince beneath her hold.

Short, Short Stories by Georgia Bin Chicken

Carol-fuelled

Karlee and I went surfing this afternoon and it was messy and onshore. There were fat take-offs and glassy walls and we surfed in a spot where no-one was. I'd had a tough day at school. Some older girls said they'd bash me up if I continued to *stick my tits out*. I hate my body. At school, everyone looks at it and most girls hate me for it. My body feels like it's its own person. Its own entity. It puts a big red bullseye on me and I don't even know which direction everyone is going to shoot from. Like it was made for porn magazines or something and I'm trapped inside it like a little kid who still loves My Little Ponies. I wear boys' t-shirts and boys' shorts most of the time to try and cover it all. Nothing seems to cover it all.

One of my friends told me I was getting a *reputation* today and it stung like a bluebottle. I feel ashamed of myself getting this said *reputation* but I really don't understand what it was that I did. Wish I was a guy. Guys don't get *reputations*. I've stopped walking to the toilets and the canteen now. It's just not worth leaving my sitting area. I feel anxious and gross until I get to the beach where nobody can see my body under the water and it's just Karlee and me surfing. But, god, there was this left-hander that came through just before and I stayed standing all the way to shore and I swear to god after that ride I jumped off into clouds and all of that shit at school just fell away. I was flying. Salty. Clean.

We sung Christmas carols all surf and it wasn't even Christmas. Even did a little turn on a wave! Karlee did heaps of turns; she'll probably be pro one day. Then we played touch footy in the sand with an old shoe. A miscellaneous shoe that gave us so many hours of miscellaneous fun. I laughed 'til I almost spewed. My hair tie snapped and my hair was like an octopus over my face. I really do have a lot of hair. Our parents were very, very late picking us up and I remember we were so hungry and it was getting dark but we didn't care. We lay in our wetsuits, half in lapping water and half in muddy sand just singing as loud as we could. There was nobody else on the beach and our voices battled the waves and the wind and our own beating chests.

It was a Christmas carol I didn't even know so I just made up the words.

I've never felt so happy as I did there, in that wet sand, singing.

Show ponies

There are these undercurrents at high school. Weird rips and troughs that complicate our little group. Girls are dating guys and girls are ditching girls for guys and girls are hating on other girls for other guys liking them and girls are kissing girls just for the guys and not for themselves. It's crazy. I just try and concentrate on my subjects. High school feels like a war that's happening all around me and inside me and there's all these people fighting and trying to drag me into the blood zone. I don't care about any of it and have no armour to protect me. I can never seem to say and do the 'right' things. Nowhere feels safe anymore. Even the beach sometimes feels tense. I often say stupid things just to fit in and I don't realise the potential of my words in the mouths of others. I just want to fit in. I don't think I'll ever fit in.

There's this pack mentality that scares me the older I get. Everybody seems to latch onto the strong ones 'cause it makes them feel better, then they beat up the weak or different ones for no reason. Maybe because they're insecure. Maybe they're jealous. Maybe their own boringness feels threatened. But I assume it must feel good to tear someone apart. It seems to be a school sport these days. I don't do the bad things, but I don't stop them either. Too scared to get involved. If I'm the target, I run. Get the fuck out of there. When it's someone else, I just keep a very low profile. I'm ashamed of it. When I grow up I don't want to be shit scared anymore. I want to be bold, to be strong. I want to fast-forward to the end of it all and get to uni, where all this will disappear.

I went to Karlee's after school this arvo. We grabbed our boards and skated down to the beach. The waves were fat and tiny but we had fun. Karlee and I were the only ones out again and there were dolphins. One of them came so close it almost knocked me off my board. We shit ourselves at first 'cause we thought they were sharks. We surfed with them for hours and it was unreal. I didn't think about school once. You know when the air is really fresh but the sun kinda bakes your skin like the top of a scone and you feel golden? That's what it felt like this afternoon. There was a super fresh smell about it all and the mist just sat above the sea like a hat. I guess that's autumn for you.

We want to get T-Shirts made that say *I heart PB*. Pambula Beach. The best spot in the world. Just before we got out, there were these weird little blue crabs that swam up and tickled our feet when we sat on our boards. They liked my feet better than Karlee's. Whenever one tickled my foot I squealed and fell off my board and Karlee laughed so hard. I think they'll nip me, but they never do. They're probably just saying hello.

When we finished surfing, we waited for ages to be picked up. Our feet were cold on the asphalt and it was like lots of tiny needles when we ran on it. We invented a game called 'show ponies'. My god, I've never laughed so hard. We were fully in our steamers, galloping around the dirt carpark like horses. We each perfected some tricks and gave each other scores. We grunted and snorted and kicked and flicked and cantered better than any horse I've seen. And every time a car drove past we would pretend we were stretching, like *normal* people. When dad finally came to pick us up my feet were numb and my wetsuit was dry and my cheeks burnt from laughing.

Scratched and skipping

Why am I so disgusting? Why am I such a loser? Why was I born? Why can't I be like everyone else? Why does everyone hate me?

I hate me.

Air bubble

Today I was surfing on a clubby board and got stuck in a rip. Like a *huge* rip. Karlee wasn't out, just me and all the good surfers. The surf was way too big for me. I'd dared myself and wanted to feel something, but when I got out there and felt myself being sucked towards the rocks, panic fizzed through me. Never felt anything like it. Like this huge painful air bubble had floated up from my chest, up my neck, up through my face and into my brain. And even though the surf club had taught me what to do a thousand times, the panic had my brain completely fogged. Couldn't think at all. My board got washed away. I dived down, deep down to the sand and tried to wait for the big white somersaults to pass but forgot which way was up. My head hit the ground and I lost myself. My body floated to the top somehow and I looked for a lifeline. One more wave and I was done. Absolutely goneskis.

'Oi! You OK?' A cheeky face beamed back. He pushed my board back towards me. I tried to suck in air, even though I was pretty much drowned. 'Hold on to your board. Don't let go of your board, OK?'

I nodded but should have said *help*. I said *thank you* but should have said *save me*. He paddled off and as he went my whole life flashed before my eyes ... my dancing class, my books, my friends, my bowl of Corn Flakes that morning. I held onto that board, paddled like an Energizer bunny towards the beach, and eventually washed in with my eyes shut. I did not let go. At school my friends told me that guy's name was Riley. He was over in the middle of the quad sitting with Danny and Ash. Didn't know how to thank him. Never had someone save my life before.

Sharky

Today I surfed at Pambula Beach and Karlee was away with her family. Riley was out. It was just us. My Dad was on patrol down near the flags.

We surfed for hours and then just as dusk came, Riley started paddling towards shore, laughing.

'Heading in next wave, George, so you'll be out here alone with the shark ...'

I laughed too but there had been a dark shadow under my

board when I paddled up a wave, but I dismissed the thought 'cause Riley was there. Riley was really funny. Often late in the day it was just him and me out and we would watch the gulls smash into the water around us, catching little fish. I'd spend the whole time laughing and he never ran out of funny material. Basically, I just stayed out to laugh and often forgot to catch a wave.

'Fuck, Riley, if I get eaten, it's all your fault!'

I didn't want to act weak in front of him. I wanted him to think I was ballsy even though he'd now saved my life twice. If I was him, I'd tell me to stop surfing ... *Georgia, you're a bloody liability.* But he never did. He encouraged me and entertained me. I tried to show off for him but always ended up looking silly. I remember the sound of both of us laughing, and how real the silhouette of that shark had become after Riley got out. The minute his feet touched the sand it was right under me. The sun went behind the clouds and the shape followed me as I went for waves. Tried catching them but my fear was so poisonous in my chest and head I couldn't catch anything. The shark alarm sounded and my dad was furiously waving at me to come in. I never caught a wave in. Ended up paddling all the way into the shore ... the slowest paddle of my life.

Riley was killed the next day in a car accident. Bleeding in the brain. His last words hung next to me. The world had turned me completely inside out.

And I wished that shark had eaten me. Wished that shark ate me so that Riley would have been distracted or derailed so that his road went another way. Wished I could have traded places with him. I can still feel that shark following me.

I owed Riley my life. Twice. And in that darkness I found Ash. And we broke apart together.

Cycles, circles, rhythms

Karlee and I rode our bikes in circles round Culgoa Crescent almost every day. Like the earth, gradually rotating, we could spin for hours. We wouldn't get dizzy because we would be so lost in chatter. It would be blowing stupidly, it would be raining and lashing, and we would ride. Sometimes it'd be so cold riding down to check the surf we'd wear our steamers underneath our trackies, with Ugg boots, but still our teeth would chatter. Some days it'd be so hot we would get our necks cooked like two sausages. We would fall into bindi patches in the summer. I knew those patches better than Karlee because I fell more. The crackle of them in dead summer was unforgiving.

I always borrowed Karlee's sister's bike and it was smooth with gears that slid like a dream. Sometimes our circles widened, sometimes they were so small we didn't move the handlebars; they were locked and we would lean as long as our stomachs would allow. Apart from the spray paint down the drain, we left no marks – you know, other than the laughter that shook the air and the bindis still stuck to my skin. The weather was always a good friend of ours.

Sometimes we'd skate and we'd go up and down the driveway pretending it was a proper half pipe 'til there was no skin left on our knees. Sometimes our wounds looked like pizzas and we'd rip off our Band-Aids to let the fresh air in. Fresh air heals everything. Fresh air and salt water.

And now I'm 18, I know those afternoons of just hanging and skating and riding and surfing are coming to an end. Karlee's got the weight of the world hanging over her body. She knows this might be the last time too. I look at my hands shaking on the handlebar and feel that Pambula Beach sun and wind on my body, mellowing me. The world shifts underneath us and we ride back up the driveway and rest the two bikes against the brick wall. I look back at the bike as if I'm losing my best friend.

On the drive north, my belongings in suitcases, I know my parents won't be picking me up from the surf anymore. There's no surf where I am going. No bike, no skateboard, no coastal breeze. Just a dream I yanked off a shelf. Not even sure if it's really mine or someone else's.

Cars will kill you

Nobody reads for comprehension anymore. Short, sharp jabs of information, that's all anyone wants. Headlines. Sexy ones. Our memories are short these days. Mine's even shorter now.

Two years after Riley died, I rocketed off the side of a cliff in a car. A huge gumtree smashed into the dashboard, which then smashed into me. That ol' bleeding in the brain feeling. Déjà vu. I was in the passenger seat and I was upside down and everything smelled of blood. I died that day. I watched it all from the clouds. I told myself what to do. Once I told myself to let go, my body was a ragdoll. A doll that I struggled to recognise. They kept yelling, *Georgia, stay awake!* but I checked out. There was blood outside and inside and the car was like old tinsel, flaking and falling over the embankment. Spinning. I heard it. Smelt it. Tasted it. It was death. No doubt about it.

Two, it's fucking two

I sat on that white bed. My gown exposed my whole back and bum. For once I felt no shame; I didn't know. The catheter and tubes and awkward sling over my shoulder not even a blip on my radar. The lady in uniform stood in front of me. 'How many fingers am I holding up?'

I looked at her annoying fingers. I knew I should know the answer. The simplicity of it was obvious.

'I'll say it again, Georgia, how many fingers am I holding up?'

I looked at my dad and saw the devastation on his face. The last thing I'd ever wanted was to make my dad feel like that. It's a horrifying feeling staring at a couple of fingers and not knowing how to count or even what the hell numbers are. All I'd ever valued was my brain and it was now mush. What else was there? I looked back at her twiddling fingers and said 'June'. That's an answer to something. And that something would just have to do. Everyone was looking at me as if they knew me, but I am not 'me' anymore, I am someone else. And I couldn't find the words to tell them that.

One day I'll know all the answers. I'll know more than that patronising lady. I'll learn to read. Teach myself to walk properly again. Learn to speak properly again. And I'll show her. Anyone that makes me feel this stupid over the next few years, I'll show them.

Me thinking this made the present somewhat endurable. But deep down, I knew I probably wouldn't show her anything. She'd written my worth on that piece of paper. It was done. Recorded. Judged. I looked at her face as she wrote on her clipboard and all I imagined her writing was *Failed. Nil. Nada.*

My pride was a baton and I fair-dinkum belted myself with it for a long time.

My self-pity was a baton and I fair-dinkum belted myself with it for a long time.

My paranoia was a baton and I fair-dinkum belted myself with it for a long time.

I had a brain injury, did you know? I repeat myself a lot.

One eighth

You know, it's a cycle they want to keep you in. I know what it's like to be so addicted to sleeping tablets you don't fully wake up for years. To be banned from pharmacies and wear this sleepy, empty shell of shame every day. To get anxiety attacks at the door of a pharmacy, for fear another pharmacy has told them that you're a dirty addict full of pharmaceuticals. To have everyone around you not know you're only one eighth there and judge you as if your whole self is there, as if you're at full capacity. And when they've decided what you are, they keep you there. It's very hard to clamber out of that place.

Magma me

I know that incense the priest jiggles around a church better than most and I'm only 21. I can smell it when I close my eyes. I smell it every night as I'm going to sleep. Maybe it will never leave me. Soaked and stained all the way into my sad skin. There's only so much death a person can take before they become too scared to live. Sometimes death can seem like a walk in the park, compared to the brutality of living. The world's on crack. No-one's safe.

And then you become bitter at others who live. You see their hideously tropical photos online and you burn. Social media is like heroin. I know it's bad for me but I physically can't stop scrolling. What am I looking for? Everyone else's happinesses? What do I do with all of it? I like it. I like it. I double click. I wait in a dark room and get angrier and angrier. And then ... well, you're so angry you can't even sing. Can't surf. Can't socialise ... you pull up your tentacles and push out. You swell. A volcanic island, just out there raging. You lose everything. You lose everyone.

Scratched and skipping

Why am I so disgusting? Why am I such a loser? Why was I born? Why can't I be like everyone else? Why does everyone hate me?

I hate me.

Sisyphus releases the rock

I didn't take time off from university after my accident. All the reports, neurologists and case workers said I had all these problems, all this residual damage. I decided I would prove them wrong. I would. At night I would cry over my teaching textbooks, all the words blurring into each other, but I thought it would all be worth it in the end. And eventually I went for my dream job and got it. But the job ended up being too big. Too big for a first-year out. Too big for me.

The boss had decided that she'd change it up this year. Take a risk. So, I became her guinea pig. I adopted the weird pedagogy that was her baby, chucked out what I'd learnt at uni and in my pracs and did everything backwards and upside down. I didn't excel. I flailed.

Towards the end, my own black tunnel was so profound that I couldn't even physically mark the kids' books. They were perfect as the kids had them. I'd surely ruin them if I touched them. My feet didn't want to walk out of that building but my gut churned at the thought of going back in. I loved those kids but I was inside out again and my blood had started to curdle. I could smell myself turning rancid. And from then on, that dream was a glass splinter in a closed fist.

And in front of you here I open that fist and watch that bloody shard tinkle onto the ground. Because that dream was never actually mine to hold. And as I watch it shine in the sun in front of me, the blood on it dries and I remember who I was before I got derailed.

Us

Ash and I had a bad argument tonight. We were watching the news and I said I didn't think refugees should be allowed into Australia. I felt all this anger and shame froth up from my gut and sit in my throat. I'd been unemployed for such a long time and I said Ash just couldn't understand how it felt to get so many rejections in the mail. Wanting to blame the accident but knowing it was actually my fault. I was just unlovable, unworthy, unemployable. I said there were not enough jobs in this country for *us*. He flinched at the word 'us' and I knew whatever this was needed to end. Silence was better than this. I'd worked really hard for this degree and I deserved to get whatever job became available. My boyfriend was upset. I was upset. I knew he was being ridiculous. Refugees were an 'other' we did not have the resources to accommodate. My boyfriend thinking we could upset me to my core. What was going on across the seas did not concern me. I had enough to worry about.

Choose-your-own-adventure

Today I started a new degree at the University of Wollongong. When I looked around at all the students who had got the starting time and place wrong as well as me, I knew I was where I was meant to be. Slightly out of place, scruffy, keen, anxious, damaged, but I was not alone. None of us were afraid of the dark. We had our own lights. Our own battles twitching across our cheeks. We had our own beat. And our pens out.

Tectonic plates and fault lines

I was sitting in an unused lecture hall this afternoon eating my lunch and a whole group of people wandered in. They ruined my peace. A panel was set up in front of me and I considered relocating. But it was raining outside so my options were limited. *Urgh*, I said. *Refugee shit, again ...* My rightness made me itch. My leftness glued my feet to the ground.

One of the panellists talked about the boat, that vessel that carried her across the water to here. A wooden little thing. Vomit and piss everywhere. All the way from Cambodia. Her mother was with her. She was nine at the time. I tried to drink my juice and eat my sandwich and just listen to my own thoughts about writing and cheese and cheese and writing. *Happy thoughts, Georgia, just happy thoughts.*

I don't want to tell this story for her. So, I will tell it for me.

I remember she was a professional, owned her own legal business nearby or something like that. She talked a lot about her mum, her mum and the suicide pill that camped like a scorpion in her pocket. It was to take if they were intercepted. As she talked, I could almost see that lethal scorpion, its nippers and hooked barb glowing through the sea mist. There was one pill for the mum and one for her. Her voice wavered in this bit and it caught my attention. I was not chewing my sandwich properly and it was kind of stuck in my throat. That woman talked about her mum and her armed pocket with so much clarity and compassion that I could hear her loaded voice and I could see that dirty corner of the boat where they sat. I could see the mum showing her own daughter that scorpion and inspecting its poisonous barb as if it was a humbug. That boiled treat that could end her life in seconds.

Reluctantly I decided, *this lady should be a writer ... what a story*. But when I looked up at her I saw something in her that I felt deep in me and I realised this wasn't just a story. This was really important. It was a kind of terror I could empathise with. A fear of death. A fear of your parents' death. A fear of the world. I could hear her mother's voice straining through the wind and sea. I saw this professional before me once again as a little girl, confused, crying for her mother ... not that different to a little girl I knew inside of me. Terrified of dying. Terrified of her loved ones dying. Unable to sleep.

'Death is not the worst thing that can happen', she said. 'There are far worse things than death.'

Far worse things than death? OK. I held my crumby Glad Wrap in a tight fist. There was nothing worse than death. I stood up, suddenly itchy and hot. The woman continued talking about the things that are far worse than death, like the things they had fled ... to seeing her mother beaten. To seeing her father tortured. To feeling famine in her bones. Watching the town she'd grown up in get obliterated. To finding out that her friends had disappeared. My inner child squirmed. I spun. Perhaps there were worse things than death.

The woman said this community had given her a second chance. She talked about gratitude.

I met that woman. I had a cheese sandwich stuck like a mouse in my throat when I met her. But I shook her hand, feeling a shame that knocked through my entire body right down to my shoes and then out across the carpeted floor. The universe felt it. I know it did. I felt the tectonic plates around my body's core shift. The plates shifted so violently they caused a fault line right through my centre. A fault line that ended up so stressed I had an earthquake of my very own. And in the shocks that followed for days after, in every single one, I felt my own evil potential. Every time I looked in the mirror, I could see a deep ugliness I hadn't seen before. But I did not look away. I owned it and I let myself change.

Fear is a mighty king

Everyone around me is being made redundant. I learnt that word from the movies but now I am feeling the full effects of it. I'm an empath and this environment is crushing. I want to fix everything. Make everyone feel better but I have no control. I see the efficiency of it. It's all being sold to me really well. But I feel the rippling and sinking effects of it through the town.

The town around me, like the rest of the world, has more people in it than before. It has changed from the one I grew up in. There is still a ripper bit of twine that binds us all together and a joy to being known and acknowledged – with smallness comes comfort. But there seems to be a growing disconnect. People watch others speak so aggressively online that I think they are frightened to speak at all. They keep to themselves. They protect themselves, and in doing so lose their connection with those around them. But the larger community is also becoming fragmented; they are selling each other off for a digitised other. A more cost-effective other. And even though everyone is given a microphone these days, it seems like only the really loud ones are heard. Everyone else has stopped listening.

I watch my friend pack up her desk. She shakes as she grabs the pens I've stared at so many times with writer's block and throws them into her box of things. There goes her purple heart-covered mug. There goes her bamboo in its indigo pot that she always claimed was lucky. There goes the photo of her kids.

She is the trustworthy face that people have cried to, connected with, turned to when things were rough. I can hardly look at her face now because I can feel everything that is written there. I return to my keyboard and clack away through the churning of my gut and the crinkling of my forehead and the world and all its wrongness. Everyone is scared. Scared of communicating. Scared of listening. Scared of losing their job. Scared for the future. Scared of each other. Hell, I'm scared. And I think the government has an easier time controlling people when everyone is scared. People do the strangest things when they're scared. And if we're scared of each other then we don't have to care about each other.

The double E's of freedom and greed

Six black elephants sit around my computer as I work. They have the blackest of black holes beside their trunks from where their ivory was wrenched. That memory is kind of like in Harry Potter when they pour the tears into the pensieve and go back through time through someone else's memory. There are hazy bits, bits that have been tampered with, bits that don't make sense – there's a magical but quite frightening feel about them all.

Every time I look at those hacked-at elephants I'm playing my own Beatie Bow. And every time, the scariest part of it lies not in the time travel or the mysteries but in humans and their demons. I can still see that man's long-faced loneliness. I remember the darknesses in each corner. And that flame robin, stuck behind glass, watching me.

Divergence

Before the car crash, my brain was in one piece. The connections were infinite and uninterrupted. They lit up like a game show and I was winning. *Ting! Ting! Ting!* After the haemorrhages, my brain felt like a cake, cut up, devoured, crumbling. My thoughts and ideas limped along the stems and found only cul-de-sacs. They would die there waiting for someone to find them. That place bled where it wasn't meant to. There was no sun to dry it out. There were no tour guides or signs. There weren't any game show lights left on. It was a dark place. At times I thought it must be the darkest place on earth.

Can you imagine one small brain bleeding in three different places? *Name* and *Georgia* were disconnected. *No* and *yes* had swapped seats. Body movements had become mathematical and mathematics was always a foreign language to me. Where is the foot? How do I alternate? What does alternate mean? That's a weird word ... All I ever heard was my own electricity fizzling out and my own heart throwing itself against the rib wall. *Fizz. Whack. Fizz. Whack.*

I'd grown up surrounded by disability and I had my own complicated relationship with the term. Now I was the one sitting in the disability advisor's office. Now I was the one needing extra help. Now I was in rehab every week at the hospital. Now I was being driven everywhere by the community transport car, listening to people talk about colostomy bags and horoscopes. Now I was incontinent. And I was mortified.

An invisible disability, they call it. Many friends defriended me. Because I was *carrying on*. I looked fine. They didn't see the scrambled-egg insides of my brain. I didn't tell them the truth because I knew there wasn't a safe space in which to air anything that dark or problematic. The darkness felt like a vortex swirling me down towards it. It felt powerful. I had very little strength left to refuse it. Some days I had none.

Our muscles have memories. Even when we can't register them, our body gravitates towards the things it has loved before. When there was nothing in that wounded brain, my body remembered familiarity. My skin knew what yours felt like. I couldn't remember our relationship but my body did. The curves of your fingers when they curled into mine. The low range of your voice that sometimes was hard to decipher. My ears didn't know the words but they loved the sound. Isn't it magical how the human body can love when the mind can't?

I couldn't write or speak properly at the time but in my old notebook I had written (in the messiest of handwriting):

My body found you
My body found you
My body found you when I couldn't

And I suppose there is no greater love letter I can offer than that. That I will always find my way back to you. Even when this world has torn me to pieces, my pieces will blow in the wind until they land at your feet.

I had nothing and no-one to trust other than my senses. And they proved pretty sound. My eyes ran over the river like it was music. My eyes had sunken into that green silk before. They knew all the animals that lived under there. My skin knew it was cold. My eyes knew that they'd traced those rocks and mangroves before. My feet remembered those mangrove roots were like little swords to tread on. My fingers had caught those crabs before. My nose could smell the salt and gums already from way up here, confined on my day bed. I didn't have to move my broken bones to feel it all again.

Then you said to me, *Georgia, darkness has no power. It is not a vortex or a hole you can fall into. Darkness has no agency. Darkness is merely the absence of light. That is all it is. That is all it is.*

And in time that is all it became, until the day I realised that human beings actually emit their own light. We actually do glow ... not just in some fitting book conclusion, but in real life. Apparently more so in the afternoons. Detectable with super sensitive cameras.

So my body produces its own light. My body held my memories for me until I was ready for them. My body loved when I couldn't. My body is a medium. My body is a time traveller. My body has secrets. My body is a survivor. My body far exceeds my mind. My body is mine. My body is splendid. What a vehicle to travel in.

15 years later and the fizz and the whacking have faded. My road works and excavating have removed much of the rubble. There are detour signs everywhere. I put them there myself. Not efficient, but they get me there, eventually. My brain has finally checked my body, identified it, inspected the bones that grew when the others were shattered, executed a risk assessment and strategic plan and I now declare the renovations over. I'm in business.

I didn't need to be thrown out like that social worker said. I just needed time. And some new signs. And I can tell you, there's a lot to be said for taking the scenic route.

Always birds

Every night when I shut my eyes and I'm just about to fall into sleep, my subconscious mind takes me to places from my past.

Last night I found myself in the damp corner of my nan's laundry. I was hanging my swimmers on a little green rope to dry. I could smell all of the dampness and hear the drip of water in the metal sink. That nan died when I was 10. I was living with her when she died and I still remember our last conversation. She knew it was our last. There were drops of sun across her doona and her skin was yellow. But I could still see her somewhere in there flickering like a neon light at an old fairground. I didn't sit down. I did not know it was our last conversation. I remember thinking at the time, *man, she really loves me, but I've got a friend's sleepover to get to. Come on, Nan.*

I walk through the laundry, imagining all the golden memories of that house threading through and shimmering down the walls, dripping onto the tiles and into the earth. Bursting up through the purple, pink and white sweet peas climbing up the back fence.

I try to look for meaning in the damp laundry and the hanging of my swimmers but I can't find any. I often go back to that house in my mind. I'm not sure why.

The places I go back to aren't always nothing moments though. Sometimes they are right before the car collides with the guardrail. Sometimes they are in the grass with my baby chickens, watching my dad's face as he drives down the driveway. Nobody had to tell me what happened ... I knew my cousin and best friend had died. It was in the way he pulled to a stop next to me, in the way he avoided my look; bad news has a weight to it you cannot hide.

Sometimes the places I go back to are unknown, back to before I can remember. Long grass up to my armpits. A goat with funny ears. A half-eaten apple. A horse bite on my palm. Sometimes

I catch myself falling asleep with the place still in my mind. Sometimes I just dream of birds. Of flying. Falling when I realise I am not a bird. Then flying again when I find my wings.

One day

I could never understand why I was drawn to fiction. Dad was a hardcore historian and revelled in non-fiction. History is so important, I know ... but then today, a friend said to me over the phone, 'Mate, non-fiction is about the facts and fiction is about the truth, come on, you know that!'

I didn't do anything for the rest of the day, just so I could unpack that.

The truth was, I had got to 30 and really wished just for one day where I could have everyone I'd ever lost back. Just to sit with them. Hug them. Listen to them. Hear that laughter again. To watch them run along the sand. Listen to their stories out in the surf. Pick fruit from their orchard. Paint sweet peas with them. To organise their recipes into categories. Laugh at their jokes. Shoot hoops with them at Top Fun. Smell those cooking smells and feel their knitted jumpers against my skin. Hear them play music. To sweep their freshly-cut hair up off the tiles. Drive around the beaches, gossiping in the car. Just for one day, drink tea with them and break Scotch Fingers in half. To just look at each other and share a meal. Just to study again those familiar lines and dimples and freckles and piercings and powder and crinkles of a face I loved. Just to smell that smell that is uniquely theirs. To hold in my hands again clothes they have washed and folded ever so neatly. Just to wake up to their big machinery rattling to life out on the dirt road. To be given just one day where they could meet my child and watch him run around the backyard, so full of energy that never seems to run out.

I wish for just one day when all of time ceases to exist and the day goes forever. And the garden blooms like it is spring. And the water falls like there is no drought. And the earth cools and repairs itself. And all the animals that have become extinct are here, walking the soil and swimming the seas. One day when money doesn't control everything, our hearts do. One day when all the things I never said, are said. One day where the leaders of the world are inspiring, kind, creative, collaborative and care about the future, not just their own political term. I wish for one day where all the people I thought I should have been, I am. One day when the fringes become the centre. And all the things I ever felt compress into one little green shoot and it rises up and blossoms. And the loves I thought I'd lost were actually not lost at all.

That day is fiction ... and that day makes more sense to me than anything else.

The great purge

By now it feels like I've sweat out everything that was in me. My whole past has drizzled out into my clothing and into this thick Indian air. Madurai is sparkly. The buildings are bright like candy and half finished. The basin fills and I soak my clothes in there like bodies, like dead selves from my past. I can hear the chanting from the city centre echo up the hill and move into my room through the window. Like a chord. Like a kite.

I've come to volunteer. To listen. To record stories. To heal myself somehow with every sweat drop and pen stroke.

And I do listen to their stories, day in and day out. Stories from the mouths of babes. But these are no bedtime stories. They would make the hairs on your leg quiver. They could make a boulder weep. The translator never shows emotion, the words are just given to me like pills on a plate.

I study the children's faces. Sadness does not flicker there as I'm used to seeing it. There is a hardness that I cannot read, but when it softens, holy smokes, it softens. Those teethy smiles that could blind a fool. The stories they tell me are ones of rejection, abuse, terror. But none of that is on their faces. Nothing that fucked up could stick to those bursting cheeks. The kids move their heads side to side, unsure of me, the stranger. But also pumped. Excited to be seen, to be heard. Sometimes they use their hands to emphasise. I scrawl, never quick enough, never good enough. My notes don't make sense, but my body always remembers how it felt. It doesn't matter how much time passes. Stories change you. There is no doubt about it. Stories change you. *So listen.*

They laugh at my camera. Touch the sequins on my shirt. Dance with their knees and elbows and own beats. There is nothing really material here other than the cloth on their backs and their bedding. Their beds are holes in the earth. Bedding is torn silk. My bare feet are deep in dirt.

And when it's time, we must return back to where we came from. Back to where we started. And would we do it all again? All the loving, all the songs we rocked out to. All the millions of stories that wove our beds together. Of course we would. I'm convinced now that everything else is just weather.

Thumb

I look down at his face, all mucousy and red. This baby-having thing was always a dream. It was never actually going to happen to me. And now I feel like someone is going to come and take him from me. Like everyone knows I don't deserve him. I'm on edge all the time, thinking he's going to vanish. Escape. Leave me. Fall. I feel like I'm always in emergency mode, waiting. Scared to really live. Waiting for another thing to be taken from me.

The Milky Way smiles and blinks and demands attention. *Look at me, look at me. This is infinite. There is no obstacle between me and you. No smog. No cloud. Just me winking down at you.*

And I realise I am all dust and stars too. And so is he. And for the first time the notion of infinity does not scare me. It warms me with its twinkly blanket … And if this is all I'm meant for, then good! He is my new, and my own, constellation. I've always needed a gentle love and it's here, this first point of contact, his hand squeezing my tired thumb. That strong heartbeat of the earth goes through us, the drum of it unmistakable, and I remember then how lucky we are to love – for whatever time we are granted.

The Tender Insides of an Orange

There's a dead body in my backyard. Before I fell asleep last night, I saw it in the shadows. I was shocked at how dead it had become. I don't know what I expected it to do. But all these years have passed and I've aged and I thought it would fall over or something. But it's still standing there, with its woody bones grabbing at the air. Those roots, like empty cicada shells, must feel so worthless there in that rich soil.

We drove back from Wollongong yesterday and our belongings are all still sitting in bags and boxes. No furniture yet, so we slept on the floor. It's amazing how hard the floor is; I always remembered it being soft. But my god, it is hard. And the walls are hard. And the kitchen is dirty. And the roaches are active. The mice peep out of every crevice. I learnt last night that they like to throw parties at night – in the kitchen, but also in most rooms. They have running races. My face felt tampered with when I woke. Grotty little buggers. Why had we moved?

In front of me is an empty backyard, not a thing alive except the grass. And even then, it's patchy. In the centre of the backyard stands the dead tree. You've never seen a deader thing in your life. It kinda looks like how I feel on the inside. My body has always been a hoarder and one thing I've learnt about hoarding is that it leaves little room for living. I remember a tenant a few years back asked for the tree to be removed. *It's well dead*, she said, *well dead*. I would have none of it. It was part of my story and therefore it must be kept, even if it had carked it. I couldn't lose another thing …

Renovation. What a time. Hard and brutal. Each wall and trellis and panel that was removed was like someone cutting up my insides and chewing on them slowly. I struggled to imagine the house, Nan's house, any other way. I wish we'd started fresh. I wish we'd bought something else. Something new. The sticky lino and dusty carpet were ripped up. That whistling kettle even melted into the old stove one night when we'd drunk too much DOM Bénédictine and passed out. Melted all the way through to the ground. The stove and kettle and lino and carpet were taken to the tip in a grand exodus. The stink of the burnt metal and plastic lingered. The flies disappeared, thank god. And against everything we stood for, we poisoned the mice. I can still hear them busily tearing apart those packets through the night. I drifted in and out of mouse-teeth dreams. Black plagues. Long tails disappearing around the corners. Beady eyes staring through the heritage cracks. Green pellets being gnawed at. I can still hear the ruffle of those cardboard packets under the second-hand furniture. The guilt of it so rampant. But then it all starts to change ...

Floorboards begin to shine. The roof is given skylights and the sun jumps in and shimmies through the house. A back deck appears with brand new steps. New paint licks the walls and expands the rooms. And Georgia falls pregnant (I know, I was shocked too!) and the air in the old house finally starts to clear.

Georgia walks out into the backyard and she spies something in the dead tree she hadn't seen before. Something in its deadness she had overlooked. Every root except one has recoiled, pulled itself entirely out of the soil, spent. Given up. It is dry, empty. Hollow. The ends of the branches are grey and brittle and scratchy. But that root, the one still in the ground, might be connected to something. As she lopes on down to Mitre 10, the dew of the grass wetting her socks and shoes, she calls her mum.

'Hey Mum, the super dead tree in the backyard ... can you remember what it used to be?'

'Mmm? Well, it was a long time ago, Georgia ... I think Dad planted it. Pretty sure it was ... an orange. He made marmalade a few times with it. Beautiful fruit. Very sweet ...'

So, Ed had dug a hole. He dropped the sprig of orange blossom in carefully. He built the soil up around it and watered it. The act of planting something so new returned a missing sense of self to him. He'd lost the majority of Ed somewhere in PNG – and that's the thing about war, it takes things from you and never gives them back.

Every second day Georgia watered the dead body. She didn't look for life in it, she just sank into the rhythm of loving it. Unconditionally. Even in drought she watered it with old bath water. She did this for two years. Now, two years is a long time to actually water a dead thing, but it was her penance. Every time she watered it, she thought of all the things she hadn't watered through her life. All the times she should have visited her loved ones but instead went surfing. She remembers one afternoon after Nan had moved into the nursing home, she actually did work up the motivation to visit her. Her and Nan walked up one of the aisles so Nan could stretch her legs. A little scraggly dog called Wanda followed stoically behind. Not much was said between the two women, because Georgia was thinking of surfing and Nan was thinking of the blister on her foot. But they both noticed a couple of closed doors with pictures hanging on them. The pictures were blue with a red and yellow hot air balloon floating in the middle through some curly clouds. You know, the clip art type. Nan didn't say anything about the pictures, she just gazed up silently at them as she hobbled by.

On her way out of the nursing home, Georgia asked the lady at the front desk what the go was with the hot air balloons.

'Well, when a client has passed away, we place a picture of a hot air balloon on the door to show the room is being cleared.'

Georgia didn't thank her or say goodbye. She just ran out the door and didn't go back in. As if death would catch her. She had always felt it running behind her; sometimes she could feel its cold breath on her neck. Georgia adjusts the hose nozzle so it is a gentler spray outward and she tries to lower it over the one haggard root still connected to the ground. She looks at the root for a long time until it warps. Such a frayed rope; how does it still manage to tether that balloon to the earth? She relaxes a little. But maybe that is just how it is. Everything must die. That's the natural way of things. And then we float ...

One morning as she waters it, she remembers back to a lifetime ago, when she moved and started uni up in the city. She strutted into her pokey room, same as all the others. One bed. One slightly damaged desk. One upright cupboard. One hand basin. One old-arse mirror. One window. All the deafening, hysterical voices outside, meeting for the first time, drunk on the O-Week energy already. She felt jubilant. She didn't look like all the others in Canberra. Georgia was messy and tanned and listened to Rage Against the Machine. But she didn't mind; this was the start of an exciting venture into adulthood, into new learning, into independence, into finding out who she was away from a small town and away from her family. For Nana, moving into her nursing home room, it was all similar – one bed. One mirror. One banal room ... they were two women at opposite ends of the rope. Georgia remembers pressing play on Nan's tape player just so Johnny Cash could fill the room and Nan could remember who she was. Everyone took her flowers, brought photos to put around the room, knitted her blankets, but the beeps and the cries outside reminded them that this was something else. This was the room that would one day have its own hot air balloon picture hanging on it. And Georgia knew that when she walked out of that room. And so did Nan.

This tree is so ridiculously dead. But Georgia keeps watering it, thinking about Nan's hot air balloon that she wasn't even there to see. She drifted through that funeral as if it was a beach day and she was about to go surfing. Knowing her, it probably was and she probably did. But by then, she'd seen so much death in her short life it had almost become numbing. Like there was this continual sombre mood over her and she wasn't allowed to laugh anymore. Even when Georgia was out at sea, sometimes she could feel death tapping on her shoulder. She was always the furthest out. Often too far out. But she felt safer out there, further away from the *tap, tap*. Every time she'd get dumped or dragged or held under she would think, *OK, here it is, here it is. It's time* ... and all of that shit she had held onto inside her body would finally keep her down there on the bottom, like a weight belt, like a boulder. But someone always saved her. Something always brought her to the surface.

Georgia always looked for a manual on how to do it, how to start living. God, she even became a librarian so she could find it. In her sleep she walked up and down rows of books. Endless aisles of books. Higher than her. Wider than her. Infinite. Like the sea. Perhaps she found all those people she lost somewhere out there past the waves, when she was alone, sitting on her board watching the eagles and gulls above her, feeling the fizz and pop of the moving salt against her body. Grief was the only manual in her short life that she had studied in detail and it sucked, but she couldn't find another one.

I stand, hose pointed right at the base, and I watch the water puddle become a dam. I shut my eyes and imagine all the space out there in the universe where all those millions and millions of hot air balloons go to drift. OK, that's enough water, enough for today. I wonder how long I can go on for like this, watering death as if it will wake up. Perhaps it'll go like this – a shimmery thread that snakes through the earth's crust, something like hope, finds its way through the hard rock, through the burning lava, through the sediments, through the layers and layers of bones and petals and autumn leaves and tears and bangs and blood of war, and keeps pushing through until it finds the surface. I know when it hits the clay it'll glide. I know when it hits fresh air it'll fly ...

Now there's fire closing in on all sides and the smoke is inescapable. I drag my kinky hose over to the dead body and I'm not just looking for my grandfather anymore. I'm desperately looking for the meaning of life. If I'm going to be in this weird post-apocalyptic scenery then I will not feel shame at asking this dead stump to answer my existential crisis. At this point, with all these red skies, bug-like aircraft, and these awkward P2 masks that don't seal very well, me talking to a tree seems the least of my problems. I don't just water the roots now, I water everything, everywhere – god forbid we'll get an ember attack.

Every news channel shows my home from various sides. Destruction above and below and by god, it's now coming from the west too. The only place to run is the ocean. I can't see my garden anymore. I can't even see the stump from the back deck. There is no daylight. Just blood red darkness. I drop my garden hose and head inside where I can breathe better. I used to whinge about my little town, but now I'd lose limbs to protect it. The world seems to have forgotten us. For months, the darkness hovers. I'm being tested more than ever before. All the darkness from my past is clouding around the doors and windows, thumping to get in. I vow to stop watering in a week if I'm still here. The anxiety in my body has formed its own news channels ...

Well, I can't begin to tell you how much rain we've had. Bucket loads. Trailer loads. Truck loads. It just keeps coming. It feels diluvian, epic. Bridges have started to fall and one man almost drowned. As the rain hammers down, all the apps show the fires fading and then later disappearing off the map, but I don't feel the same. Even some brave birds have started to sing but their songs are different, not as long or as bright. Everything has started to green up and it looks fab, but I've been rearranged again and my insides aren't working properly. Out of nowhere a virus descends on the world like a cape and everyone seems blinded. Everyone looks at everyone else as if they are diseased and we all become separated. I want to believe in magic and I want to believe in science, but more than anything I want to believe in people again.

That's the worst part of it all. Everyone's just full of hatred and fear. And anger, don't forget anger. I'm fucking furious that I watered that stupid dead tree for so long. What a goddamn waste of time and energy. Maybe the dark spaces of a human heart are the only spaces. Maybe there is no good. Maybe there was no point to all this …

Well, it's finally a sunny day, with no fires! We head to the beach, my husband, my dog, my son and me. We stay far away from everyone because social distancing is mandatory. I sink into the water as if I'm made of lead. As if I am one big fired bullet, full of bad energy and hoarded nothings. I hurtle through the water. Cumbersome. Heavy. I just keep walking until the whitewash covers me and I am immersed. And then the whitewash clears and all that's left is sand and blue. My hair, like weed, drifts around me. I'm suspended in some sort of limbo. Neither here nor there. Neither up nor down. And somewhere underneath that water, my body remembers who I used to be. What this used to feel like. I start to see. I see my son's kicking little legs as he learns to swim. I watch the hundreds of bubbles float upwards from his toes. My husband's gentle hands around him prop him up, sometimes helping, sometimes letting go. His little feet kick and kick and kick and kick. And I never ever want those little feet to give up. I don't think I've seen anything so amazing as those little feet under the water kicking, half floating, half sinking. His muffled laughs saunter through the ocean waves and find my ears. Little kicks. Bubbles. Little kicks. Laughter. And it's here I start to realise my body isn't heavy at all. I am no bullet. And I am not stuck on the sand. He squeals with laughter as he learns to point his toes, and the flurry of energy and bubbles blocks my view. And that's the manual. That's the manual I've been searching for. It wasn't on a dusty bookshelf. It wasn't on the news. It was right in front of me. Sink. Kick. Float. Laugh. Repeat.

I pick up the hose again. It's been a while. The plastic nozzle is in my hand and it no longer feels like penance. It feels like a rhythm. Like a prayer. Like a real connection.

The fictional character, Georgia, walks out to hang my towels over the back deck to dry. She picks up the hose again and stands in position, watering that root. She hasn't given up. I had, but not her. That's the beauty of fiction and art, I suppose. It's much easier to believe in things there, where the goodness of humanity always triumphs and everything makes sense in the end. But then I see it. After many, many years of watering a dead stump, I see an unmistakable green sprig on the end of that brittle branch. The orange tree is actually alive! There it bloody is! Georgia laughs. I laugh. And all the past softens. Ice in the sun. It drips onto the ground and soaks the earth.

That orange tree produces its first fruit in over 20 years and reveals to the new world what an orange used to look like, used to smell like, used to taste like, back before pesticides and hormones and mass production measures. Georgia feels this spirit unfurl in her heart like a fern frond. Unravel like a tea leaf. It tings like a triangle. She feels it boom like a kick drum. It pops and loops down her limbs like a gymnastic ribbon. It opens its hand to hers and she holds it. I hold it. This new wave pulses through my system and helps me see colour in everything. Lego colour, bold, bright. Mesmerising like Magic Eye. Textured like a jungle. I can hear boppy melodies, Nintendo 64 melodies. I can feel my joints pump up with WD-40 and I feel more air push into my lungs than I thought they could hold. I want to run. To fly. And I realise for certain that nature can rebuild itself, if we let it.

I shut my eyes and the smell of orange blossom laces the air with security … that I'm not scared anymore. I am living in colour. I know where I came from, I know where I am and I know in the future, if I need to, I can bring back the dead.

As my son *brrrrs* and *bip-bips* around the honeysuckle on his little digger, watching the bees, Georgia waters that tree not just with water, but with tenderness. Something the yard hasn't felt in a long time. Something, perhaps, the world has forgotten. Something I know my own body has been aching for, from me. My body has stored everything for me until I was ready. And I know there are things in it that don't need to be there anymore. The time for cleaning and decluttering has finally arrived.

Georgia nods to me as she fertilises the orange tree. She places fairies around its roots to dance. She tells me to start painting again. And then, almost without warning, Georgia gently hands the hose back to me. I don't know why I burst into tears when I take it from her.

'It's time.' She waves as she disappears through the hole in the back fence.

And I let her go. But it doesn't feel like grief this time. More like shedding a skin. And though I can't see it, I can distinctly hear the tinkle of a flame robin somewhere very near.

To sleep is to float is to forgive

Dying is so much like going to sleep. I must start with water. I am water. I've died in water 23 times in 23 different dreams. I've almost died in water for real, three different times. I've almost died just from the darkness many, many times. I've died before and that is why I'm an insomniac. I have died in my dreams too many times to count. But I've died in a car once. For real.

When I died it was like involuntary sleep. I thought of every visual and memorable moment of my life to date – frantically flicked through my memories like a rack of clothing in an op shop. And every night that frantic shuffling of coat hangers laden with food and tears and dances stops me falling into slumber. It wakes me up and up and up and up until I am iridescent on the roof, stuck to my own tongue, trembling in my ears, petrified like a rock, I am alight —

I cannot sleep then. I am not ready to die. This is what I said when I died. This is what I pleaded with my maker. And I was coercive. And now I won't sleep and I won't die, and if my heart rate increases enough with this Graves disease perhaps

I'll transcend my own fruity body and become a hummingbird, flapping and flicking like a blinking eye. Quick. Light. Moving so fast I stay in the same spot. Grounded. But lidless. Without lids, the lenses dry out and the water drinks all of my shame. And it's impossible to sleep. The water drinks me down in gulps too loud and I eat all of the sleeps I never had. As if they were a protein that could rebuild me, as if they were fillers for the voids left by all that dying.

You can't fill those voids.

You can try to drown them, but they burst to the top every time. Obsessed with floating. Why are the death bullets in me unsinkable? And even if I am dead, even if I one day get to sleep, these floats will pick me up on the way and take me with them. Every. Single. Time. Those air bubbles drag me screaming through the currents and tides towards the sky. I pop out like a bottle. A messageless bottle, but unsinkable all the same.

There I am: floating on the sea lip as if it's the only valuable thing. Water my life source, my body, my home. And one day, when I'm ready to stop flying, I'll land there. With the ibises and the egrets. Touching my own cotton plume and knowing I am water. And when I die, it is nothing but a small sleep and a float upwards until I am water, in water, of water. Even if I am lidless.

By that stage,
I'll just want to go home.

When I was a teenager and my body changed and had headlights all over it and my chest grew into something else, I felt dirty. I was lit up even in the shadows and the only thing that washed off that shame and slime was salt water. It was the only thing that could clean me up. Shame that rife has an acidic sting to it that really rips apart a teenager's skin. The salt water with its magic alkalinity could take that sting away. It made my body weightless. It covered my indecent curves. It was only on land that I didn't recognise myself.

Only later did I realise my curves were real curves, like a nautilus shell, like the waves, like a wing. I would never call these curves anything like that again. With their buoyancy they brought me to the surface even when I was well and truly drowning. They fed hunger. They protected me from my obsession with conformity and showed me the beauty of the fringes. This body is of this land and this land is extraordinary. Let's stop stuffing them up.

I am no longer waiting for your approval.

I will rebel with water and tenderness – that is how we save a life.

And I've got used to going to sleep now ... I found my lids.

And at least when I do eventually die again, I will die as myself —

I will end back where I started: of water, of land, of feathers. Floating and flying through time, and

silvery threads, and space junk, and sand, and hot air
balloons, and flocks of birds I do belong with, and
sticky lino and whistling kettles, past hatching swan
eggs, and trees planted by loved ones well before my
time, and through pubs and schools and memories
and houses and wetlands and blood. And I will hear
nothing but the flame robin as it flies freely beside
me.

You see, I've made peace with my earthquakes ... and
I've made peace with my hand in all these fires and
I know now how to change my ways. I know how it
felt to stand in those rains that came after the flames.
I waited until that shame washed off completely, and
I let myself soak all the way through to the bone ...
until I was indeed water again.

> I know when this house falls down
> the earth will always catch me.
> And even if you don't know it
> I know it will catch you too.
> You are already forgiven.
> You will find all of your stories there
> waiting for you.

Acknowledgements

First off, to my Facebook friends and social media networks: THANK YOU! You threw me lifelines and important words when I needed them most. You will find yourselves throughout these pages.

Thank you to Dr Josh Dubrau for sharing your cleverness and literary prowess with me. You helped shape this beast beautifully. An enormous thank you to my incredible, kind, sharp and savvy editor Jess Magrath. Thank you for being a wise and trusty voice in a long, dark tunnel of a year. You, my friend, are superb. Thank you to Matilda Gould for your keen eyes, expertise and generosity. Your contributions here have been immensely appreciated. Thank you to Bronwyn Mehan and the team at Spineless Wonders for supporting me yet again and bringing these stories to the page. SW RULES! A giant thank you also to Bettina Kaiser and Heike Krieger of BKA+D for the innovative overall aesthetic and illustrations within *Dear Ibis*. In my experience, collaborations between artists are one of life's most exciting experiences and they have the most rewarding end products. *Dear Ibis* has been no exception. Special thanks to Toby Davidson for his guidance and advice on Empire (Part One). Special thanks also to the Bega Aboriginal Lands Council, in particular Graeme Moore, for your invaluable lessons on Country. Thank you also to Gary Lonesborough for your incredible storytelling. Let's yarn again soon. Thank you to Alexandra Seddon for changing my little world through community building, conservation and kindness. Panboola is my second home. Thank you to Dorothy Witt, Lisa Ballantyne, Sam Mills, Andrea Johnson, Darcy Tranter-Cook, Gary

Lonesborough (Jnr) and my mum, Margaret Liston, for kindly reading these pieces at various stages and offering sage advice. Thank you to my Bulldozers & Associates who have revived me and brought me back to surfing, positivity and just hanging out. Thank you to Kristie Lee who jumped into that surfing bubble with me right back at age 13. It was fun, mate. Thank you to Alycia Collins who has grounded me and loved me for over thirty years. You, my friend, are beautiful. Thank you to Gabbie Stroud, Gary Lonesborough (Jnr), Meghan Brewster and Rosie Lourde for being you and being fabulous! What an incredible support team! Thank you to my family and in particular Dad, Mum, Lis, Joey, Jake and Lil, who have always been there for me. And thank you to all my friends throughout the years who have brought me joy.

The biggest thank you goes to my husband Sam and my two boys Ashie and River. You guys make my life sparkle every day. Thank you for the lessons, love and life you share with me. Thank you also to my dog Charlie, Terry the chook and all the wild and wonderful birds that frequent my backyard, because even when I am alone, I'm not really alone. And thank you to you the reader. Thank you for investing in me and allowing me to tell you stories. It was and is always a great privilege.

Further Reading for Empire (Part One)

Blay, J. On Track: *Searching out the Bundian Way*, 2015.

Conrad, J. *The Secret Agent*, 1907.

Conrad, J. *Heart of Darkness*, 1899.

Donaldson, S., & Norman, S. *Koori Heritage Stories*, 2012.

Egloff, B., Peterson, N., & Wesson, S. *Biamanga and Gulaga: Aboriginal Cultural Association with the Biamanga and Gulaga National Parks*, 2005.

Lawson, H. *While the Billy Boils*, 1896.

Lawson, H. *At the Beating of a Drum*, 1910.

Lawson, H., & Patterson, B., poems published in '*The Bulletin Debate*' between 1892-1894.

Lawson, H. *The Loaded Dog*, 1901.

McKenna, M. *Searching for Blackfellas' Point*, 2002.

Mead, T. *Empire of Straw*, 1944.

Pascoe, B. *Salt*, 2019.

Webb, F. *A Drum for Ben Boyd*, in Davidson, T. (ed.) *Collected Poems: Frances Webb*, 2011.

Webb, F. *At Twofold Bay*, in Davidson, T. (ed.) *Collected Poems: Frances Webb*, 2011.

Webb, F. *Henry Lawson*, in Davidson, T. (ed.) *Collected Poems: Frances Webb*, 2011.

Webb, F. *Senior Hirsch and the God*, in Davidson, T. (ed.) *Collected Poems: Frances Webb*, 2011.

Glossary

Balawan: Thaua name for Mount Imlay, a culturally significant mountain located in the Mount Imlay National Park outside Eden.

Brylcreem: Hairstyling product for men.

Connie Wackers, lick their dackers: A derogatory and colloquial slogan directed towards Catholic school students usually by public school kids. Connie is short for convent. Dackers is an informal term for underwear.

Gunyahs: Thaua word meaning shelter or hut.

Pannikin: A cup or drinking vessel.

Wigwam for a goose's bridle: An old English colloquial saying that became popular in Australia in the early 1900s meaning 'none of your business' or used as a response to an unwelcome question.

Wreck of Hesperus: Emanating from the poem 'The Wreck of the Hesperus' by American poet Henry Wadsworth Longfellow, this colloquial and popular saying means 'untidy, dishevelled or in a ruined state.'